SIMPLY SEPARATE PEOPLE, TWO

LYNN CRAWFORD

SIMPLY SEPARATE PEOPLE, TWO

BLACK SQUARE EDITIONS & THE BROOKLYN RAIL
NEW YORK, NEW YORK
2011

Simply Separate People, Two, 2011
Copyright © 2011 Lynn Crawford
COVER IMAGE: *Chameleon and
the charm bracelet: sacred hearts,* 1997
Copyright © Valerie Parks
Oil on linen; 12 x 12 inches

DESIGN BY: Shari DeGraw

ISBN: 1-934029-20-3
ISBN 13: 978-1-934029-20-6

BSE & TBR are distributed by SPD:
Small Press Distribution
1341 Seventh Street
Berkeley, California 94710

1-800-869-7553
orders@spdbooks.org
www.spdbooks.org

The Brooklyn Rail
99 Commercial Street No. 15
Brooklyn, New York 11222
blacksquare@brooklynrail.org

*...how life, from being made up of little
separate incidents which one lived one by one,
became curled and whole like a wave...*
VIRGINIA WOOLF

CONTENTS

PROLOGUE 11

1 BRY 15

1.5 HARVEST 33

2 BRY 91

2.5 THE TURN OF THE NORTH 109

3 BRY 149

for
Harry Mathews, Lynne Tillman, and John Yau,
Simply Special People

PROLOGUE

Gertrude Janine
(Trudy)

My mother, a classical actress, named me Gertrude Janine. She explained, from as young an age as I can remember, I was given that name in honor of a kind neighbor who helped her through a troubled childhood. But from the first time I attended *Hamlet,* I believed otherwise. My mother has a history of performing impish acts, then feigning innocence. So when I saw the play *Hamlet,* which was on a junior high school field trip, and encountered Gertrude, that character, I felt the warm, prickly force of betrayal. To make things worse: my mother played the role of Gertrude; my mother was the entire reason our class went to see the play. She not only had the acting role, but also arranged our school's free tickets and bus transportation.

The response of my classmates? Because I was named Gertrude but (thank you Mom) called Trudy, they did not have any reason to connect my name with that questionable character. And they thought it was impressive to have a parent who stood tall and received attention for something as unusual as acting.

After I saw the performance, I read and re-read the play, focusing on the character I believed to be my namesake, Gertrude. The weak, easily-led Gertrude. This was the sort of mischief I understood my mother to make: she would say she had named me after someone beloved since childhood, when actually naming me after a famous literary figure, and not a heroine. When I asked my mom how could she name me after such an awful woman, she answered that I should not judge Shakespeare's character so harshly, especially since I have never been a wife, a mother, a widow or queen. And that the Gertrude she named me after was not that literary character (who on stage she had played to acclaim, though long after I was born), but a kind neighbor whose last will and testament allowed my mother a large amount of money.

My mother had a rough childhood. Over the years I have heard the stories. Lack of parental attention, dirty floors and sinks, shabby clothing. A father who came home late, drunk, and smelling of perfume; a mother who responded by taking up nighttime gardening.

"Your grandmother was a gentle woman, but a ferocious gardener," my mother told me. "She channeled her sadness and humiliation of being cheated on and poor, of having the sickliest farm animals in the county, into making and caring for her garden. No one could ever figure out when she did it, but I can tell you: she did it at night. I heard her go outside. Father, either drunk or passed-out, on the couch or floor, never heard her. But I heard. I watched from her bedroom window. If the night was pitch black I could not see, but knew she was working hard because I heard her breathe, grunt. But if there was a full moon or a starry sky I could see. And it was astonishing to watch her little body crouch, dig, rise, cut, snip, groom. All day long she was busy with regular farm jobs: feeding animals, picking fruit, digging vegetables, bathing children. But at night she worked on her own plot of land, turning it into something remarkably pretty. On the other hand, gardening was tough on her looks, giving her a deeply bent back and hunched shoulders.

"She never had time for me, her only daughter, but our neighbor, Gertrude, did. Gertrude saw that I was uncared for. She saw that I did not like being outside or doing the dirty farm jobs. So she took me in. She taught me how to knit, sew, wash, and bake. My mother was never one to spend time inside. Gertrude gave me small jobs (drying dishes, darning socks, polishing silver) and paid me enough to buy toothpaste, shoes, and notebooks.

"That is the woman you are named after, Trudy. If it were not for her I never would have gone to drama school, I would never have gone onto become a classical actress. If you do not believe me, there is nothing more for me to say."

This is a very, very good story. But if you knew my mother the way I know my mother, you may not believe it. You may still wonder if you were named after the weak literary character. I could travel to my mom's town, or telephone people from there. I could ask around, check records to learn if a woman named Gertrude lived anywhere near my grandparents. But that would mean dealing with data. And one thing I learned from my mother is this: finding and facing facts is not necessarily an approach that provides you with a serious advantage, enriches your position, or lands you any closer to contentment.

I
BRY

What you say, and do not mean,
follows you close behind
BEN HARPER

Late morning. The children play with blocks, our apartment is in order, I sit at the kitchen table documenting in my new journal. The journal is sturdy, lined, leather-bound. It is a birthday present from my father-in-law, Jorje. In the past, I documented in the spiral-bound notebooks one might buy in harshly lit, crowded drugstores. Because of their flimsiness, one could rip out pages, cross out words, even entire passages. I rarely did that. My documentation style: think through thoughts, put them down. I tend not to jot down fragments and later construct them into coherent sentences. People who write creatively, or write simply to cleanse thoughts from their head, can work this way. I write to record information. Recording in this volume, with its heft and sensation of permanence, feels different, more serious. The journal is a home appliance, not a transportable object to carry in my purse or tote bag.

Three years ago we come to this big city. We are my husband, Euge, and I; my husband's father, Jorje; our older twins and our good friend Trowt – a chef, now working outside the city in the country. I give birth to our younger twins within weeks of our relocation. Now they are three years old.

With the move, elements of my landscape change beyond the expanded nuclear family. As I documented back then, my husband and I were born in a farmland community. We grew up in a period that saw partial transition toward modernization. The citizens of that region, a combination of farms and new subdivisions, have a particular way of life. Eating and dressing patterns reflect long hours of heavy labor: large meals, sturdy shoes and layers of loose clothes.

Some of these habits are still practical. I mentioned that we have residents who farm for a living. They include old families, struggling to hold onto deteriorating barns and rusty equipment. We are also home to a newer group of farmers who, sensing the market for grass-fed beef, organic eggs and produce, approach farming in a way that includes changing technologies. These residents have college degrees, some in agriculture, but others in disciplines outside that field. Some have worked as lawyers, teachers, waiters, actors or nannies. What links them together is faith in sustainable agriculture. They are convinced that this form of crop growing is best for the environment, and that it generates the highest quality meat, fruit, vegetables, and dairy. They believe all residents should buy organic, and when possible, local organic. They display and distribute EAT YOUR VIEW buttons and bumper stickers.

Even though our hometown supports this small, but hopefully growing, group of farmers, farming is not central to our economy, the way it was in the last century.

The countryside and weather remain the same. Flat landscapes, bitingly cold and windy winters, blisteringly hot summers. But now cars, and multiple other motorized vehicles, indoor heating and air conditioning offset that severity.

We continue to be community oriented. Visiting the small downtown, open markets, churches, developed strip malls and supermarkets, means seeing familiar faces and stopping to chat. By familiar faces I mean people who have lived here, and known one another, for generations. As I mentioned earlier, residents dress in bulky layers, and not just the ones who work rugged jobs. Professionals who drive to jobs and work in an office or shop still wear heavy boots, protective hats and weighty outerwear. This style is practical if you spend days working the land, walking through fields, along roads, riding a horse to reach neighbors or towns, grow food in your fields and garden to cook and bake things like stews, soups and breads from scratch in the kitchen. These clothes are not so practical if you lead a sedentary, indoor existence.

On the one hand, I find residents' attachment to outdated patterns of dressing and eating somewhat touching. It is touching to see the doctor travel to his office in a well-equipped jeep, dressed in a padded vest and weighty boots; touching to see the banker eat a breakfast fit for the life his cattle-driving father led: eggs, bacon, peppers, potatoes, cup after cup of strong coffee. It can be touching, but sadly so, to see a tradition hold, especially when the reason for the tradition dies out. There is some discomfort in viewing all of this reaching backwards. I do understand the urge can be hard to resist. Reaching backwards is a seductive, if deceptive, reassurance. As my friend Trowt puts it, "Nostalgia, its mighty tentacles."

2

When Euge, the kids and I first move to this city, I am struck by all of the well-dressed, thin people speaking multiple languages, the underground and ground transportation, by how exhausting it can be to do an errand: walk several blocks, climb up and down stairs, cross hectic intersections, switch trains – movements especially difficult when lugging children and packages. If we use a car here, it is usually for a weekend event, such as driving out to visit our friends in the country.

Differences between home and city life shift the way I think, eat, and dress. So do changes in another space: my body. Childbirth jumbles hormones. For months after giving birth my physical and thinking patterns are unfamiliar. Moods fluctuate with frightening intensity. Same with things I do and do not want. I dislike remembering how hopeless and feeble I felt back then, just after our younger twins were born. I dislike taking myself back to that jittery, panicked mindset: one minute I cannot bear to be divided from my babies, the next I feel an urge toward separation, the next I dread that any physical division will shatter all three of us. Night and day I press my ear to our infants' chests and mouths, checking breathing. I lock all the windows, fearing I will throw one or both of the newborn twins out of one.

Sometimes I find comfort in having extended family and friends around. Other times, their presence, seeming to barge into my personal territory, is unbearable.

The level of dependence my babies and I develop for one another at once rivets me and worries me into believing that mothering is a life-eating form of energy.

That deep, dark period lasts for months. Then comes the less frightening but still glum, gray period. I, by all accounts a practical, active person, wrestle with large and small decisions. How much time should I spend with the newborns, how much time should close friends and family members spend with them? Breast-feeding, yes, but should I suckle the infants separately or together? Is there a case for introducing formula?

When the twins are slightly older: should I cook and make a paste of their food, or buy the (highly rated by parenting magazines) organic puree sold in jars at the "better" markets? At what age do you start lessons? Which lessons? What about germs in public parks; the sand they run their fingers through, and sometimes taste, the playground equipment they climb and touch? What about the potential danger of outdoor pets, dogs especially, but also cats? And people now own, and walk, snakes, birds, ferrets. And there is wildlife. Can squirrels be rabid? At what age do you allow play dates? How communicable are childhood diseases? How much alone time do young ones need; how much protection from weather; how much sleep during the day?

Choking on food or toys is a hazard. And there is always the balance of safety vs. developmental tool. One example: the playpens we used when our older twins were young are now considered unhealthy. What is healthy is allowing children to roam: unstructured movement is an excellent learning device and provides solid preparation for trips to public spaces. Yet such freedom requires careful supervision, which the playpen does not.

I am saying, with the playpen a parent gets a break. Sometimes you need that break to use the bathroom or get something to eat or even to do something less urgent like pluck an eyebrow, apply blush or lipstick, leaf through a magazine.

Over time, I come to believe that my worries and fears are in fact realistic concerns acknowledging the challenges present in our world. I begin to believe this after talking regularly with a counselor. I stopped seeing her when she had a baby and went on maternity leave. Now, looking back, I do not agree with every direction she took me. I see she tilted things toward an extreme opinion.

"That woman is an enabler," warned my father-in-law, Jorje.

Still, I believe that my conversations with her helped me shift out of the bleak period, into the gray, glum one.

How did I find her? Contacted the counseling service advertised in the information package that came with my hospital discharge material.

3

On the upside, she helped me whittle down and articulate my worries to these three:

Babies are absorbing.

It is my responsibility to make sure they grow up happy.

This world is one dangerous place.

My counselor heightened awareness of my strengths. Even when in my deepest dumps, I loved my nuclear family unit (I've since learned many postpartum mothers cannot stand the smell of their husbands and the children of others).

She also helped me understand – and I hinted at this earlier – that intelligent parenting requires living in constant terror. It is the inept parent who sails blissfully along, the competent parent who cannot. The competent parent cannot ignore the presence of pollution, drugs, food allergies, natural disasters, crime and other dangers in our culture. Cannot ignore the fact that apparently pleasant people in parks, groceries, recreation and learning centers, might in fact be predators. Caregivers must teach children to be fearful of cars, scooters, bikes, strangers, wild and domestic animals. My counselor helped me understand that my reluctance to teach my children about these dangers stemmed from my outdated upbringing. Fine in its time, but now irrelevant to our modern world. I grew up in a much different time and place. There was a different safety level. Instilling fear in children back then would have been rude and out of place. Now, even where I grew up, parents must be aware of danger, and teach their children that awareness.

Just now, I remember sitting in the hospital bed shortly after giving birth. The staff is off with the twins, checking vital signs, Euge and the older twins are downstairs, eating in the café. I am, just for a moment, alone. My still unfamiliar body issues strange odors, and thick sweat. I am jammed with worry, remembering one snowy Christmas Eve, as a young child riding in a red sleigh with my cousins, drawn by a horse with my uncle at the reins. We have just eaten a meal of rib roast and potatoes, brownies and peppermints. A thick blizzard fills the gaping spaces between our warm house and us. My cousins and I, beneath blankets, nestle into each other and the hay, enjoying the cold ride, looking forward to the next morning when we will wake up to carefully wrapped presents under our tree. It is a perfect moment, a perfect mood, and it is that kind of combination of comfort and excitement I'm wanting to offer our children, but do not believe that I can.

Jorje was – and still is – benevolently skeptical about those sessions with the counselor. He applauds my motivation. He understands that isolation can generate unhealthy thought and behavior patterns. Speaking with a professional rather than an intimate can diminish feelings of despair and disconnection. Sometimes, it is asking too much to share such fears and anxieties with a good friend or family member. Sometimes, you do not want that information branding lifelong, personal relationships.

On the other hand, Jorje warns that low self-esteem often goes hand in hand with working in a care-giving profession. He cautions me to be wary of any advice given by this counselor, however much I admire her.

One thing we, Jorje and I, agree on: You cannot predict the results of the child rearing process. That process may be long-term rewarding if you do it right, long-term devastating if you do it wrong, or even devastating if you do it right. You just have to keep your head down like a plough horse, experience things day by day. Do not look to the side or too far ahead. Do not panic.

Our older twins turn out to be fine. When we move to the city, we worry how they will function away from the tight-knit community they grew up in. But both immediately take to their new life. They enroll in a university, live in a dorm but visit us frequently, study drama, write and produce plays and perform well in the city's busy and competitive artistic environment. This is a great comfort to Euge, Jorje and me. We love these young grown-ups. We are relieved and proud to see them thrive.

But, as anyone who read my earlier documentation knows, the older twins are not biologically connected to me, and to be honest, it worries me that they are so successful, in part, because of this.

4

I have loved my husband Euge since childhood. It took him a longer while to notice me.

He likes it here, in this urban expanse, though he frequently visits our land, stables and house back home. I, too, visit home, but not as frequently as he does.

Navigating this big, dirty city requires feeling lonesome and brave. Maybe this is what cowboys or pioneers experienced as they plotted their courses through empty western spaces.

Euge is an outdoorsman back home. However, he enjoys this urban center, especially his job here, I am sure, because he is able to incorporate his knowledge of the outdoors in his life here. He is the head guide at an immense indoor activities association. The club has horses, lakes, stables, rivers, cliffs, ski areas, and offers classes on cabin building, stargazing, astronomy, rafting, fishing and hunting. Euge is the only guide certified to teach members to train, ride, and whisper to horses. The management relies on him to keep activities and classes realistic. When Euge mentions in a programming meeting that he misses the weird and wonderful fragrance of a river at night, management enlists his help in matching that smell to the club's rushing, indoor river. They consult him on the species and number of freshwater fish to stock their river with. On Euge's recommendation, they install beds of sod teeming with worms next to the river, allowing club members to kneel down and dig for their bait.

Tonight, Euge teaches a technique-focused fly-casting workshop. I am up on our apartment's roof with a group of city-based family and friends. Sun shines, wind blows, a dirty river sparkles in the distance.

Last year Jorje had a long, shallow pool installed on the rooftop of our apartment building. He designed it to emit fresh aquatic fragrances. I am up there with the three year olds, who sleep under the protective umbrellas of our double jogging stroller. Jorje and his colleague, The Assistant, just finished a swim after a hot game of tennis (Jorje lost). We sip fruit flavored water, The Assistant grills sausage, Jorje squats next to me giving his anti-furniture lecture. "Sitting on furniture, standing still and playing aggressive organized sports all add up to back problems. If you love sports and your job requires you to stand still, you can offset some of the damage by not using furniture. Squatting is healthier, sitting on the floor is healthier…" He trails off.

The Assistant and I have heard this before, we know we will hear it again. Jorje's striking girlfriend, Bitty, a stage actress, walks onto the roof carrying a script and wearing spiky mules and sunglasses. We all stand up from whatever we are sitting or squatting on. She kisses me, The Assistant, then Jorje. "Darling." She continues, in an audible whisper, "Put your shirt on. I can see those muscles from fifty feet away and it is distracting. I've got lines to learn." He nuzzles her neck. I try to decide if I am eavesdropping or if this is just an intentionally loud whisper.

The rich smell of sausage permeates the roof. Bitty, a furniture user despite Jorje's warnings, sits on a chair, slips off her pink and ivory mules. "Bingo," says The Assistant, flipping sausages, piling onions on top. "Anyone for a plate of perfectly cooked food?" I decline. Jorje and The Assistant will share the meal, save some for the older twins, sure to stop by soon. Bitty, preparing for a role, might take a few bites from Jorje's plate.

I love listening to Bitty explain her approach to dramatic roles. Today she talks about the challenge of imagining small and concrete things about her character. For example: underwear type; chosen snack; hygiene habits, table manners; daily activities; what kind of sheets does she sleep on? As she talks, Jorje examines a serious blister formed around and underneath a callous in the middle of his left palm, his racquet hand. Bitty says to no one in particular, "But even with all that preparation, I have doubts about this play. I mean, how do I say a line like, *Sweet things go in and come out of my mouth,* without letting mean critics, attacking my acting, rattle in my head?"

"Switch to fashion, those people never attack," suggests The Assistant, as he lays down a platter of food at Jorje's feet.

"HA," she responds.

Jorje and The Assistant figure prominently in this city's fashion industry. Fashion designers and theater directors alike can turn barbaric, to one another and their staff, particularly under the pressures of production. Same, I am learning, with some of the neighborhood parents. They really can turn barbaric. They say things like, "Good moms have to be pit bulls." As if being a pit bull – aggressively jumping, nipping, chewing – is in any way any kind of a good thing for a parent to be.

Pit bulls can be barbaric. I wonder about barbaric behavior connected to pressures of high power professions – CEO's, mayors, emergency room doctors, as opposed to the vocation of motherhood, spending days with children, yours and others, their toys and the sorts of people related to children and child activities: other mothers, teachers, doctors, television characters, singers; athletic, movement, music, and language coaches. I can understand why a CEO would need to behave like a pit bull, but not why a parent would. I wonder if this belief in parenting aggression, comparing the job to being a pit bull, is caused by personal strain, misplaced ambition or some strange combination of the two.

The older twins, who have a sixth sense for good meals, appear on the roof. They swim several laps, practice some dives, before settling down for some food and conversation.

Let me say a bit about their first play. It is about a businessman who buys up and develops beautiful beachfront property, then constructs private mansions and strip malls that clog up traffic and prevent public access to water. Citizens protest the developer's opportunistic practice. The developer, raised in a dirt-poor family, is driven to make a good life for himself, his wife and children, but learns he must think outside his immediate circle, and consider others. He transforms into a great benefactor. The twins are excellent at depicting transformation; their typical hero is a character who goes through great difficulty achieving it.

This evening our conversation turns to weather derivatives, a sort of insurance that covers damage caused by unseasonable changes in temperature, but not damage caused by natural disasters. Euge bought these derivatives for our place at home out west. We discuss the recent crazy weather and whether one should invest in the derivatives for property owned here in the city, or nearby. The three year olds wake up, eat some yogurt and banana and bits of sausage (no onion) that I carefully cut. They play with their beloved big siblings. In awhile it is time for the older twins' evening rehearsal. Euge calls to say he will be late, but not too late. After the fly casting technique workshop, he must lead a night owl spotting tour in the simulated forest. But it is an abbreviated seminar, so could I please wait up for him? The big twins kiss us all, pack up their straw slippers, towels, scripts, lotions, baseball caps, and head down to the apartment to change into dry clothing. Soon, I will take the children downstairs, put them to bed and wait for Euge to come home so he and I can share a late night drink and some of the meal The Assistant has prepared for us.

5

Next morning, when the younger twins wake up, Euge and I take them swimming on the roof. Later, he brings them to work (his club has excellent daycare) and Bitty and I walk to the older twins' rehearsal. Some days I bring the younger twins, but not this day. This day, feeling refreshingly light, I carry a square, beige perforated leather bag The Assistant gave to me years ago as a shower gift. I do not have anything inside except lipstick, keys, my cell phone and a sunglass case. My journal is not (as I mentioned) transportable. Bitty carries a roomy, slouchy pocketbook that holds her new script, a cell phone, several small notebooks, and a case filled with different kinds of makeup and creams. She is a frequent skin hydrator and makeup refresher.

In the park we pass several carefully dressed children with their parents or babysitters. I know and greet many of these people. Jorje deserves some credit for the fact that I learn (somewhat) how to socialize with the urban parents and caretakers, our new neighbors. He encourages me to engage, not cut myself off or just interact with my family and the counselor. He helps me participate in small, celebratory parties, teaches me how to buy interesting, under-priced gifts for the adults: truffle shaver, scented candle, one manicure are each unusual but good gifts. Over time, I learn to talk with the parents, at least a little bit. We sit in the park or push jogging strollers and discuss boosters, food allergies and ways to keep toys and clothes in order. At first I was not interested in socializing. I felt drawn toward isolation. "It is a totally normal and healthy way to feel," my counselor said. "Listen to your self: regroup, withdraw."

"Beans," said Jorje to her response. "I've lived enough lives and seen enough babies being born to know that isolation is just the thing a new mother does not need."

But my relationship with other parents remains slightly awkward. Talking with them can sometimes be comforting and interesting, at least until someone turns barbaric.

I notice that the more time I spend with full-time parents the more I see of their barbaric behavior. The kind you can see that might remind you of a pit bull.

What I mean about nasty, barbaric behavior are parents who speak badly about one another and speak badly about the children of others. This does not happen until they spend a lot of time with you. This does not start at once. It starts slowly, over time, and builds up. They do not speak badly about each other or badly about the children of others in front of you if they just spend time with you in small doses.

But maybe I am relieved they are barbaric because it makes me crave time alone and without time alone I would never be able to document in this journal.

Bitty and I walk down our busy street, past shops and stands overflowing with bright arrangements of food, plants and flowers, toward the church where the twins are rehearsing.

Three years ago, when Trowt and I first walked down this street, his comment on these beautifully arranged stands was this: "I travel to the best food destinations in the world. Markets filled with muddy vegetables, squawking, dirty poultry, but you clean and prepare it right and the taste is excellent. This stuff looks pretty but is in fact sapped of minerals, tasteless on its own, and requires the presence of a highly-flavored sauce or at least heavy salt."

Trowt, remember, is a chef.

Even though I have lived in this city for three years, I still feel the pressure of visual over-stimulation. There is so much to see, too much for me, I think, and I lose control over my attention. I think that is partly why I am drawn to writing projects. They help to shield the seduction of all there is to look at in this jam-packed city.

We enter the rehearsal space, which is an old church. Waiting for my eyes to adjust to the light, I feel the hushed weightiness of the building. To reach the theater, you walk down a long corridor, crisscrossed by pipes. We come to the theater. On stage, student actors sit in a semi-circle, rehearsing their lines.

"The urge to try and be charming at this age is embarrassingly high," Bitty whispers, rubbing a small amount of cream between her palms, then onto her cheeks and forehead. We sit down.

The twins' play portrays a weakened urban center, whose debilitation is attributable to poor planning. Throughout the production, it is emphasized that lack of money, people, jobs and services – plus a diffuse and outdated bureaucracy – prevent solid city construction. The play is set in a large, depopulated urban center filled with empty buildings, burned-out store fronts, shattered windows, buckled porches and caving rooftops. The conflict is between two groups: one advocates tearing all these structures down, the other lobbies for preservation of the homes and the entire downtown, especially the once-magnificent pre-depression skyscrapers.

Some call the demolition process pruning, likening the practice to pruning rosebushes. Trowt, and our other friends in the country, believe the buildings should be knocked down but reject the use of the word pruning completely. Rosebushes, while sometimes strategically planted by people, do grow in nature. Buildings are always only erected by people. They should be demolished by people, too, not pruned.

Much of the play's action takes place at a fantasized board meeting set in a surreally tall building that towers over all the other buildings in the dilapidated city. Men and women dressed in white sit at a round table, looking down at activity. The stage set has a few stark elements: lamp, table, and sleek shelves. The emcee is a tall character and has buzzed blond hair, erect posture, and wears pale green frame eyeglasses.

Seeing the rehearsal elates me, not because it is a happy story (though they tell me that in the end it is) but because it gives me so much to think about. It is now late at night of this same day and I am still thinking about it. For some reason this kind of thinking signals the end of my documentation, or at least this portion of it, because I have been thinking about different ways I might use writing to make me a better person.

I worry that as time goes on I will come to value the qualities of a pit bull. That I will become barbaric. That I will speak badly about parents and children, like some of the mothers I meet in my neighborhood. And some of these mothers I meet have other bad habits. Some, for example, just seem to be bored and desperate for company, or extreme exercise or beauty treatments or specific food regimes. Some are preoccupied with shopping or redecorating their homes. Most seem to be fantastically ambitious for their children to succeed in a way that will outshine all other children; fantastically ambitious for their children to be stronger, smarter, more beautiful, to know more musical instruments and languages and to win more sport competitions, than any of the other children. Because this conduct frightens and saddens me, and because I fear I may unintentionally adopt such potentially bad behavior patterns, I decide I must find something to do with myself besides parenting and documenting.

What follows this documentation project are pages of totally different projects; writing, unlike the documentation project you now read. A tribute to a novel that I loved as a young person, and find myself thinking about increasingly now. It is my hope that this undertaking will take me somewhere good. By good I mean to a place where I am less likely to overly focus on life's details, and where I am less likely to develop bad habits. Because my project involves writing creatively (technically rewriting), I do not use the sturdy, lined, leather-bound journal given to me by Jorje. I use the spiral-bound notebooks that you buy in crowded, harshly lit drugstores. They allow me to rip out pages, cross out words, even entire passages. I aim hard to try and get everything down just right, but I want to be prepared just in case that goal proves to be unrealistic.

1.5
HARVEST

I am not a jerk although sometimes I act like one
SPEARHEAD

Jake walks into the bar soon after getting a cavity filled that had been lingering for weeks. I had been on him to get it fixed. Jake gets involved in things he is doing and forgets to take care of himself. He is better at taking care of others.

Tonight I am out with graduate students and staff on my overseas university exchange program. Jake likes my friends. He and his group are older, kinder, and more confident. Less attached to formal education. Being overseas is nothing new to my friends, who can – proudly – recount experiences they have had with the world. Just now I hear Bo, completing his fourth masters degree, say to Gunth, a photographer in the journalism program: "I am not in this country's university to please my parents or further my career; I'm here to learn from people."

Bo follows a sparse diet; one stein of beer gets him high. Now he is tipsy, but tomorrow morning he will be up early, doing nostril-cleansing exercises and sipping herbal tea.

Bo and Gunth sit at the end of our table. We are drinking beer and discussing Hindu mythology, focusing on the beloved figure, Ganesh, with his human body and elephant head; his taste for sweets; his ability to transcribe. Ganesh is a popular adornment. Several students—Bo, his girlfriend Frances, Gunth, Siri, me—wear his image at least once in a piece of jewelry, tattoo, t-shirt or toe ring. We discuss Ganesh's origin. What it means that, according to some sources, his mother made him from the dirt of her body.

"It has got to be menstrual blood," Siri, who speaks six languages, says, bobbing her bald head, "Ganesh's mother made him out of the dirt of her body. Dirt, menstruation." Siri has an encyclopedic memory. An image of Ganesh is tattooed on the back of her right wrist.

Jake enters the bar and moves to our table with someone who impresses all of my program friends: a well-known local businesswoman, not connected to the university. She is very pretty. For an American student, this—socializing with a non-university citizen—would be a total score, a move that would impress parents, peers and faculty advisers. But Jake is not in close touch with his parents, or connected to the university. He travels regularly but lives in this country, works as a reporter, covers wars, global human rights issues, drug cartels and genocides. I know this contact with grisly events and so many forms of sadness gets to him but he rarely admits that it does.

Now he stands behind me, kisses my head, puts his hands on my shoulders, introduces his friend to our student crowd:

"Meet Sigrund. She designed Brett's place and more recently my dentist's new office where I just ran into her." This said with slightly slurred speech. "Damn numb, still, from the drugs they shoot in your mouth."

I know, like and respect Sigrund. She is a fine interior designer who did wonders with my studio apartment. Jake hired her to help me. When I moved in, over a year ago now, it was one empty, tiny, room. She suggested a loft bed with closet and storage space underneath, which makes the small place seem bizarrely roomy. Ask anyone who has been there. And the paint job and fabric touches she added made a tremendous difference. She knows how to put an interior together with an individual's personality and budget.

Sigrund, who has a beautiful set of teeth, sits down at the table. Jake, hands kneading my shoulders, listens closely to the Ganesh discussion.

Watching Siri, as she brings up Siva, Ganesh's supposed father, I totally understand why she shaves her head; her skull is a beautiful shape. "Ganesh's father cuts his head off, but he finds some way to replace it, to put a head on even if it is an animal head, so he admits, even repairs, his mistake."

After awhile, the discussion switches over to spatial organization. Sigrund says that some people mistakenly believe design is just for the theater or museum or sprawling home, but in fact it can economically enhance a dorm room, apartment, office or bungalow.

Jake leans down behind me, whispers, "Let's step out."

I know that Sigrund, a nimble marketer, will not mind us leaving her with this group.

Outside, we walk several blocks to my place. Jake's is much farther away. The street is quiet, the weather cool, and the sky nearly starless. We reach my address, climb the steps, open the door and walk inside. Jake says, "Sorry about last night and this morning, Brett."

"Why do you always have to do that? Hurt my feelings?"

"I know, Brett, I'm sorry, I can't help it. I just clam up. Clam and clench."

He leans his head back. I look up at his neck, shadowy in the streetlights coming through my bedroom window.

"Brett," he exhales.

He grips my waist; I take his face in my hands.

Jake owns two types of shirts, both white: long sleeve oxford and short sleeve tee. And he owns multiple pairs of khaki with deep side pockets: trousers and Bermuda shorts. When I first meet Jake, and see him always in the same clothes, I am interested in his closet: is it filled with multiples of the same shirt and pants, or does he just own a few of each and wash them carefully and frequently? It is the first case. Not an excessive amount of multiples, but enough to get him through a few weeks without going to the laundry, enough to last him on his trip. He rarely wears underwear. He is always very clean.

Tonight he wears a long sleeve oxford and Bermudas.

Jake can drink large quantities of alcohol but never seems to get out of control. He eats a lot too but remains fit and well-toned. He is an excellent listener, and can be a talker but always interestingly and always about things he knows: fishing, politics, food, sports. His interests, so different from mine, are appealing. What is not appealing is his habit of going away. I do not mean for work assignments. This is what I mean:

Last night he comes over late with peeled shrimp and a cold bottle of wine. We eat, drink and talk on my balcony. Then go inside. It is very good. Later, I turn toward him; he is gone. No body. This has happened before; in fact happens a lot. At these times, I hate Jake, I really do. But he always comes back, shoulders hunched over, asking if I am alone or need money. This time I cry, punch his pillow, resist the urge to call him up screaming, "You asshole!"

The next morning I keep to my routine. I do not have a scheduled class, just blocks of studying to get through. I go out to get a coffee, stop in the drugstore to buy arch supports for my jogging shoes. Just after paying for them, my friend Gunth, camera dangling from his neck, approaches:

"Your pale skin, your messy hair, your long legs, I've got to shoot."

My first concern, stronger than wondering how I look at this time of day, especially after crying all night, is to conceal my new purchase. I do not want my arch supports in the photograph. Holding them is not like holding a perfume container or a flower or a pet, objects that people often pose with. And I wear a size-11 shoe, which I am slightly embarrassed by. Even though size-11 when you are six feet tall, which I am, is proportionate. Luckily I bring the oversized tote bag, which I made myself out of bandanas, which I never normally bring out with me in the morning. But today I do, so have something to shove the arch supports inside. In fact, inside my tote bag they are hidden completely.

"So," I ask, walking out of the shop and into the park with Gunth, "what do I do, what do we do?"

"Just walk. I'll ask you some questions. By the way, this is all for my graduate thesis which, you might remember, looks at the difference between making documentaries about people I know as opposed to strangers. You, I know. But I am going to pretend I do not. So don't act as if I know the answers to questions even if we both know I do. Ok?"

"Ok."

We stroll in the park, Gunth asking me questions he knows the answers to, but we both pretend he does not. Gunth clicks his camera periodically.

"Where are you from in America; what do you teach and study? What do you find interesting about this country; are you homesick; do you have a lover?"

When we reach my place I tell him it is time for my morning run and he says I shouldn't be surprised if I see him in the bushes, shooting that too. He adds that arch supports have helped his foot pain. I look at him with irritation. "Brett," he says, "I take pictures, my eye sees everything. I didn't photograph the arch supports, don't worry, but I saw them. They will help your feet, they really, really will."

He is decent, he really, really is.

We shake hands, I enter my building, thinking, that was a good diversion from asshole Jake.

I head out for a run. Someone waits for me. Not Jake, but another, much less sympathetic asshole.

Who squats at my door, shirtless, in bunchy sweatpants, pouting, gripping a tightly rolled yoga mat but Bo. He has a girlfriend, Frances, and knows Jake, knows about Jake and I, but nevertheless follows me around wanting to talk to me about himself.

"Hey," I say. He does not stand up but stays squatting and pouting. I know this ploy for gaining attention, and refuse to bite.

"Brett" he says, finally standing up. I do not answer. Then he squats down again and bangs the back of his head against the wall, repeating, "Brett, Brett, Brett."

I bolt down the stairs and into the park, feeling guilty. I offset that, or try to, by telling myself I did a good job not enabling Bo's passive-aggressive behavior, that responding to him likely would have led to a level and type of engagement destructive to us both. Bo gets into moods. When he is in them, any way you interact is going to be unfit. In these moods, Bo wants you to ask him to talk, to really, really, really ask him. To beg. And he is a guy who, once he starts talking, can talk till you go out. He starts off not talking then you ask him what is wrong and he still does not talk and then you ask him again and he starts to talk and then he talks and talks and talks until you are completely drained from his talking. You pray for him to stop. When he does not stop you have to learn to shut him out.

I get home, exhausted and elated from my run, and am relieved to find Bo gone. I shower, settle in for a good long session of study. After awhile the bell rings. I guess correctly: Jake. I hope he is here to apologize.

Jake says he would have been here earlier but he ran into Bo sitting cross-legged on a park bench with a hangdog face. Jake asks him what is wrong. Bo answers that his book did not get reviewed in the week's paper and he is feeling low about that. He also says he worried about me because I was not in yoga class this morning.

This is Jake, spending his time listening to a person complain rather than coming over and paying attention to me after his bad behavior toward... ME. I suggest we go outside. We walk downstairs, go to the corner café, and drink cups of coffee. Jake orders a slice of cake. I wait for Jake to apologize but instead he talks about how he especially wants cake because he has a dentist appointment this evening and eating something sweet seems the right thing to do just beforehand.

This is Jake, spinning irrelevantly. I start feeling irritation.

Later, we go back to my room and it is very good. Then, just when I expect my apology he turns silent, stays lying down, staring up at the ceiling, not responding to my questions about the rest of his day.

Something shifts in my self-control. "Can't you at least grunt out some answer, rather than lie there, gaping like a barn animal?" He stands up, looks down at the floor, and pulls on his Bermudas and leaves. I throw my hairbrush at the door.

Jake is a vacater, a mental vacater, a mental vacationer. His departures leave big, black holes. He cannot help it. First he is here, then he is not, and then he comes back again. It must have something to do with his job.

Later that night, after his dentist appointment, he behaves well. Brings Sigrund, someone I like very much, to the bar, apologizes and stays warm and attentive well into the next morning. My mistake is expecting that side of his personality to last. But it is my form of hope and hope is not a bad habit to have.

"Well," my therapist (more accurately a graduate student/psycho-therapist-in-training) says when I relate this during our bi-weekly session, pressing the palms of his hands together, tapping the two index fingers against his lips, in a practiced, expressionless tone, "Surely you were drawn less to Jake that night in the bar than to your decorator friend, Sigrund. You masked unacceptable sexual fantasies toward her."

No, no and not.

This illustrates a big problem with my assigned graduate student/psycho-therapist-in-training (seeing him is a requirement for my university degree program). He leaps to his own opinions without listening to what I am saying, or how I am saying it.

A professional therapist, a good one, would probe Jake's need to blot out his actions, my insistence upon acknowledgement, my attraction to this mental vacater, my choice of university study and friends. This graduate student fixates on an aspect missing from my entire story: unacknowledged sexual fantasies.

I totally acknowledge my sexual fantasies. Toward this graduate student, no fantasies. Toward Sigrund, no fantasies. Recent fantasy examples: all my university professors and Jake.

I hear — we are a small community, and word gets around — that my graduate student/psycho-therapist-in-training has a thing for Sigrund. He is that unprofessional with me, his training client, that unable to recognize his own projections. I wish there was a way I could report him but anything I try to do could so easily implicate me in a web of transference neurosis, or at least make me seem vengeful. I admit, I can be vengeful but I do not want it documented on my student record.

There are two things with Jake and me. One, his tendency to slip away; two, our powerful connection.

I would talk to my graduate student/psycho-therapist in training about that. What draws me to and repels me from Jake with his deep-seated, need-to-exit quality. And how this personality trait works for him professionally—makes him such an excellent reporter of gruesome human behaviors—and against him emotionally—his relationship with me. And we could also examine why I once or twice sleep with Jake's friends, seedy behavior for sure, but also one strong way I can really express to Jake how much his disorder, and the big, black holes it leaves, derails me. Or at least, those liaisons seem to somehow balance out the power.

But my assigned graduate student is much more interested in manufacturing stories about me, or projecting his fantasies onto me, than listening to what I say or how I say it. Some of the students on my program are overly aware of breeding, and claim to know details of one another's lineage. Having met a selection of their parents and grandparents, I do not see how they can be so sure. I know there is intermingling within that crowd. And I know that they sleep with one another, their fitness instructors and groundskeepers. In the end, how do you really know who fathers you? Unless you are Siri, and look exactly like your dad. Last week he was here, on business, and invited some of us to his hotel suite. He begins the evening by leading a brief group meditation, followed by a round of aperitifs, wine, and a several course dinner downstairs in the hotel's four-star vegetarian restaurant. At dinner he launches into a riff against aperitif glasses: "Why would someone invent a vessel that small?" He believes the reason is all about meanness. "Mean is a good word," he continues. "It can be defined as unkind and as cheap; two qualities that are one and the same." Jake just used that word, mean, in the same context, telling me about overhearing Bo in bed with Frances. "It is a mean thing I do sometimes, listen," Jake admits.

I remember hearing Frances in verbal action. She had had too many aperitifs, and was going on, to Bo, "Do not use the word 'amusing' when you mean stupid. Just say, 'How stupid.' Or, if you want to tone it down, say, 'I do not care for'… Do not say, 'Butter is amusing,' just say I do not care for butter, or I do not care for beer.' But I hate it, Bo, when you over generalize, use the term to refer to an entire city. Like when you said 'Paris is amusing.' What you meant was 'I do not care for Paris.' You and I know, anyway, what that means. What you did not care for was this: no one took you to famous restaurants, or stores. No one reviewed your book or came to your workshops. None of that is Paris, all of it is you. Do not confuse the two. You and Paris."

This directed toward Bo. It seems harsh even now, but who can really judge any relationship? Most of us like Frances, and Bo does seem attached to her, whatever attachment means to Bo.

Jake would never serve you an aperitif in an aperitif glass. He drinks from one if someone serves him. That is part of his job, fitting into social situations. It is important for him to observe. But when on his turf he serves everyone, including himself, drinks in a sizable glass. I'm not saying he fills the glass up with more liquid than would be in an aperitif glass. He understands the logic behind the aperitif glass is that the aperitif should be a small amount of liquid. He does not quibble with the small amount of liquid. He quibbles with the meanness of a tiny glass.

2

Jake is consciously responsible. You would not find yourself carrying him home; he, on the other hand, would make sure to carry you. He would not scam you for money, but would have it for you if you needed some. He always has a job, an office, paid vacations. He always has a nice place to live, and lets friends visit any time, and live there when he is off traveling.

The night after dinner with Siri's dad, we all meet at a welcoming party for a visiting lecturer, the well-known mind-body healer/research statistician, Markus Duker.

I mentioned that Bo is working on his fourth master's degree. And he has published a novel. And religiously, rigorously, practices yoga. Bo, whatever else you can say about him, is productive. This degree he currently pursues is in the field of psychology. I am in the field too but am less interested in the statistical side than the talking cure side, that kind of therapy. Bo thinks I will never go far as a psychotherapist if I ignore statistics. I know he is probably right but I just have no head for numbers.

Markus Duker, who I have only seen in photos, is startlingly handsome. Startlingly. And he wears finely cut clothes out of nice material, the kind of clothes I see European and Middle Eastern men (and, sometimes, Americans who live and travel abroad) wear.

Yoga and meditation feature prominently in Markus Duker's psychotherapeutic methodology (something not so unusual, these days). He is exceptionally good at generating, and sustaining, buzz; a sense of something happening in ways that attract all kinds of people – mathematicians, physical and psychological therapists, yoga teachers, people generally interested in popular culture. But he also is a respected, serious, statistician; he has efficiently systematized the otherwise tedious process in specific areas of data collection. This gives him a strong following among scientists and researchers, more interested in working with data than human beings. He has a wife and three children who live in the United States. In interviews, he speaks about his family frequently, but cannot see them that often since, from what I can tell, he spends so much time traveling.

I walk into the reception, see him, dressed in a gray washed silk suit, standing in a crowd of students and faculty, looking just like his magazine and internet photos. I hear someone ask him how he has the discipline to work on something as dull as statistics when he really does not have to, having garnered so much success in his other professional areas. He laughs, "Dull? What is that? In any case, I love numbers." When he sees Bo (who I stand next to) he excuses himself from the group and extends his small, thick hand. "Bo, Bo. Bo." They shake hands, and then hug.

Bo introduces me, "Brett is an American psychology student, studying here, where her boyfriend Jake, a foreign correspondent, lives. She seriously practices yoga."

"Would that foreign correspondent named Jake have a last name and is it Barnes?"

"Yes," Bo and I say together.

"He is one of the best, if not the best," says Markus.

The three of us start to talk. Actually, Bo talks, waving his long, thin fingers through the air. He talks about how some people are great with numbers, and others are great communicators, others understand the mind/body connection, others still are great researchers, but to find all of these traits highly developed and within one person is rare. Markus smiles, comfortable with the compliment. Someone tells Bo he has a telephone call which leaves me with Markus Duker. He asks about yoga classes here, but I have a burning question to ask him: "Do you truly believe people can change?"

He nods his head vigorously.

"Do you believe yoga helps people change?"

He again nods, answers, "Think of the various ways our culture 'helps' people out of a rut—self-help manuals, diets, detox centers, plastic surgery, psychotherapy, fasting, full-blown lifestyle changes like leaving relationships, changing professions, physical relocation. It is an industry. Yoga is an industry, too, but it truly does help with change, because it gets your plumbing going, and, in truth, everything comes down to plumbing. Once that works, a person makes better decisions."

My graduate student/psycho-therapist-in-training walks in

to the gathering, turns his back to me.

Markus and I work out a time to meet for a yoga class tomorrow. Jake breathes on my shoulder.

"Damn tooth still hurts."

"Jake." I kiss his cheek.

"Ah, the boyfriend. Markus Duker, I am a fan of your articles." This said with two taps on his chest and a short bow.

The two men shake hands.

The three of us start to talk. Jake is very good at getting people to talk about what interests them. Within moments he has Markus describing his current project: compiling intimacy statistics. His data shows that the contemporary focus on intimacy is overrated. "I do not say that intimacy is overrated, just that the focus on it is; the focus on the ability to be close. As if a tight alliance is something that can happen when you make it the goal, a mission. Intimacy is a byproduct of circumstances, not a goal in itself. Industry support of intimacy as a goal in itself is an excuse for selling foolish books to people. If you and someone spend all your time letting down your guard, staring into one another's eyes and unconditionally supporting each other in letting down your guards, how can there be time to do and learn other things life has to offer? Stars, history, birds. Swimming, parachuting, chess. Cooking, music, dance. 'No, I'll pass on the Italian opera. I'd rather sit in some group seminar holding someone's hands, listening to the thing that most ashamed him/her in high school.'"

Bo joins us, "Markus, do you believe in true love?"

"Faith, blind faith, in true love is a very sinister belief."

An announcement tells us it is time for Markus Duker's address. He and Bo head toward the podium.

Jake, "He sure is dreamy."

"Once a statistician, always a…"

"But you, Brett, can convince him true love is not sinister."

"Jake…"

"Go on, then, you are good enough."

"Jake, he is just trying to get a rise, talking that way."

"You are good. More than enough. Or you could try that one," he nods to the back of the graduate student/psycho-therapist-in-training.

Jake and I look into each other's eyes, smile, and acknowledge what does not need to be said: we share a certain tenderness.

3

Jake's landlady is a small woman, thin but not frail, who dresses carefully and gives music lessons. Our now friendly relationship starts awkwardly.

Not long after I move here, Jake and I have a bad, loud, fight. I leave his home, walk a few blocks, return. On my way up the sidewalk I see his landlady standing in her window. Our eyes meet. I climb the stairs to Jake's still-open door, say in a low voice, "Ceasefire?"

"Yes, please," he says, taking my head in his hands.

"I forgot about your lady downstairs."

"Not anymore" he says, pointing out the window. There she walks down the street gracefully, erect, dressed in a fitted coat, stockings, and heels, shopping bag draped over her shoulder.

That afternoon I visit her, with flowers.

"I am very sorry if we disturbed you. We were rude and out of control. It won't happen again."

She smiles, says, "I did not like hearing your voices. However," nodding to a picture on the mantel, "my husband and I had our share of battles. He was a musician and you know how they can be."

"I do know some ways some can be, I worked in a music store," I tell her.

"Well," she says, "my musician was ardent, gifted, unreliable. We loved hard, fought hard, made up sweetly. I hope when you and Jake have your bad fights you at least make up in a way that brings you both pleasure. If the answer there is yes then your fights might help you love each other. If the answer there is no your fights are without purpose."

This starts our friendship. I often visit her, sometimes bringing flowers.

I mention this now because of something eccentric Markus does after our yoga class.

Jake invites Markus and I over for whiskey after yoga. Whiskey after yoga, a pure Jake suggestion. When Jake extends invitations like this people usually just say, "Sure," then help themselves to his well-stocked supply of spring and mineral waters.

After class Markus and I change out of drenched practice clothes, into dry street-wear (a red halter dress for me; a loose, off-white, open vest over stove-pipe jeans for him), and walk over to Jake's. On the way Markus asks about a good produce market.

Food, flowers, trees, and all forms of vegetation, I learn, are very important to Markus. He tells me that he goes out of his way to buy local organics, wherever he travels. So when he wants to stop at the market I guess it is to buy some clean fruit or unaltered bread, and am thrown when he selects a large bouquet of flowers and asks,

"What are Jake's favorite colors and scents?"

"Why, are you buying flowers for him?"

"You, are a judgmental, young, and very tall lady" he says, tapping his index finger on my nose.

Damp and dehydrated, we approach Jake's place. Both holding our duffel bags of wet practice clothes, Markus carrying, also, the flowers. He has chosen a yellow arrangement. I hope that the landlady is not home, or at least not looking out her window. Because if she is, she will expect that the flowers are for her. We ring Jake's bell, walk up the steps, he opens the door dressed in a bathrobe and slippers.

Jake is well-mannered and has a feel for comfort. He wears slippers at home, rather than socks or going barefoot. He stocks extra toothbrushes too, and bandages, cotton swabs, aspirin, lip balm. Next to his sink are interesting dispensers of soap and hand cream. Even when he travels, and he travels light, he is not without extra necessities. He is just one of those people who pulls off economy and luxury at the same time. Today, he answers the door, fresh from his shower, hair wet, a little curly around his ears. His chest is visible through the bathrobe, his muscular legs are visible between the bathrobe and slippers, but his slippers cheat us out of a view of his feet, which are well formed and high-arched, like a statue's feet.

I feel how I often feel around Jake: touched, stimulated and irritated.

"One finger or two?" he asks us, hand on the whiskey bottle.

"We'll help ourselves," I say. Then, "Jake, are you going to change?"

"Right. Be just a minute," he says, walking into his bedroom, closing the door.

Markus and I help ourselves to mineral water, sit. Markus drinks his mineral water out of a tumbler. Backwards.

"Why are you doing that?" I ask.

He bends over, takes a sip, sits back upright, says, "Most people see you drink from a glass backwards and think you are trying to get rid of hiccups. But when I do it, it is to improve the healing processes already launched in my body by a detoxifying practice such as fasting or yoga."

He again bows his head over his glass, knees pressed together, "sips," sits back up, erect.

"And you work your abdominals, too," I say.

"That would just be Bo. That man has body issues," he says.

Now, I will dish on my friend Bo with Jake, maybe even Siri, Gunth, Frances, but refuse to go there with this colleague of Bo's I barely know. And to think this Markus is a therapist! I cannot see he has any boundaries.

"That yoga class was great," I say, moving the conversation away from possible gossip. "Smooth but hard."

He says, "Yes, and the teacher did not say anything stupid. Sometimes I am distracted when teachers start talking too much, relating personal anecdotes, repeating words like 'edge' and phrases like 'personal challenge.'"

"Oh, I don't know," I say. "Some teachers are really good at weaving together anecdotes, even stories, while they direct you into postures."

"All personal taste. This class was very breath-focused and for me that is where and what yoga is: breath."

Markus finishes his mineral water, without a single spill or dribble. His cell phone rings.

"Yes? Yes. Ten minutes." He stands up, "That was Bo calling an impromptu meeting. I guess some of the statistics we compiled are inconsistent; I have to sniff out the problem. I will come back and eat with you, Jake and the rest of your gang. I do want to discuss Bo's eating habits with you."

"Gang?"

"Well what would you call yourselves?"

I let Markus out (he leaves his duffel bag and the flowers), go in Jake's room. He is lying on his bed, looking at the ceiling.

"Nice of you to join Markus and me, nice of you to let us know where you were and what is going on."

"I'm low, Brett. I'm just low."

When Jake admits his problems, my heart melts. I sit next to him on his bed, stroke his face. The room has a good chest of drawers, and good natural light because of its big windows.

I lightly knuckle, then kiss, his forehead.

"Where's your statistician?" he asks, turning away from me.

I spend a lot of time talking to the back of Jake's head, or the side of his face.

"At a meeting. I guess there were some discrepancies in the figures they compiled," I answer.

Jake has worked in war-torn places and reported on agonizing things. He says this should not and does not bother him, but I know that it does. The experiences sometimes come together and overwhelm him, shut him down. But one thing I learn about loving Jake: just because I sense something is true does not mean there is any good in me saying it.

"Brett, I am low and when I feel low I act like a jerk."

"A jerk is better than an asshole."

He turns his head halfway to me and gives a small smile.

"So now will you look at me?" I ask.

He turns his head, faces me, "Brett."

After awhile we get up and dress.

Jake puts on a clean shirt, a pair of shorts, walks into his bathroom. I wonder if he will tell me when and where he is off to next. We hear a bell. It is Markus, carrying a basket overflowing with produce. He is with Bo, Frances, Gunth and Siri.

"This country has excellent vegetables: cabbages, sprouts, cauliflower, asparagus, they — whoever cooks, citizens and chefs — just don't always know how to prepare the food," says Markus.

"But of course," says Frances, "you do. Know how to prepare the food. And, my guess is that you are planning to show us."

He answers, "I learned a lot from my friend, a chef and an organic farmer, who grows no-GMO vegetables."

"What's his name, Mr. Potato Head?" asks Siri.

She, Bo and Frances go into the kitchen to rinse vegetables.

Markus, to Jake and I in a low voice, "Now that girl, Siri, has one sense of humor. Is she single?" To the group in the kitchen, yelling, "Cut off the asparagus tips, make sure you peel the midrange stalks above the part you throw out."

Jake notices the flowers.

"The landlady is away, visiting her sister," he says.

"What?" Markus, arranging crumbling cheese over olives on a plate, asks.

"How many degrees do you have?" I ask Markus. He tells us. He has quite a few. I cannot actually keep track of his answer.

"Wow Jake," I say, "you hardly have any degrees. Bo has four. And I am working so hard on my one."

Markus says, "Degrees cost a lot of time and money. And look at Jake: satisfied professionally, financially stable."

"But degrees can be useful," I say. "For jobs, self-esteem. And you acquire things, discipline, skill, information."

"Who says you need degrees for that?" say Jake and Markus at the same time.

"Did you find out the problem with your numbers?" Jake asks Markus.

Markus beckons us close to him, speaks just above a whisper, "There was nothing wrong. Bo misread the figures. I don't think that man eats enough, it makes him lightheaded."

"Why tell us? Tell him," I say.

"Should I?" Markus asks. "But I don't know him, it might seem intrusive, rude, aggressive."

"Well if you are going to tell us, you may as well tell him, rather than talk behind his back," I say.

"Whoa, Miss high on my horse," says Jake.

"Jake," I say sharply.

"Listen, ok, I was kidding, but Markus has a point, Brett. If Bo does have a problem it is better to discuss what to do with friends who know him, rather than barge in. And Markus is his colleague, their relationship is professional."

"Ok, I'm put in my place," I say. "Maybe I don't want anyone being mean to or about Bo besides me."

"Don't forget Frances," Markus and Jake say at the same time.

That night I dream I become a dentist. Or do I dream that I married one? Or that I had several children who all grew up to be dentists?

Later that week, waiting for my graduate student/psychotherapist-in-training, I flip through American family-oriented magazines. He walks into the lobby to tell me he is ready, sees my choice of reading material. Inside his office, he closes the door, starts our "session."

"Am I to understand, then, that you and Jake are considering tying the knot?"

"You mean because I am looking at American family magazines?"

He nods.

"I like to look at American family magazines for the casserole and dip recipes, the tips on lawn care maintenance, and every other kind of article and accompanying photo because I am honestly homesick."

He nods his head, taps his forefingers against his lips, responds, "And?"

4

During the university break, we all head to a therapeutic healing convention Markus is a part of. The title, which we do not think came from Markus, is Sacred Flow = Transformation. We decide to meet the week preceding it for some rest and relaxation. We first travel by train, then take a bus up to the mountains for a few days of fishing, swimming and hiking. Our bus is full of travelers. Some speak our language, but not well. We don't speak theirs well either, except Siri. The rest of us try. Even though it is morning, they drink wine out of flasks. They ask us to share. I don't, I can't; too early, too much new altitude. I think Jake and Siri do.

We get to our hotel at night. The weather is very cold. I am unprepared. Jake, a thoughtful packer, brings extras of things I can use and wear (scarves, vests, dental floss).

Gunth, who made the hotel reservations, pre-orders a dinner he expects will meet the dietary needs of our group: green beans, peppers, potatoes, salad, soup, apple cake. He also orders chicken, explaining to the kitchen that some, but not all, of our group is vegetarian. The kitchen did not understand this specification, and loaded up each plate with vegetables and chicken in the kitchen. As the waiter approaches with individual plates of food, each topped with a drumstick, Bo waves his hand, coughs into his napkin, shakes his head no.

"I'll take it," offers Jake, lifting the leg off a pile of beans and peppers.

"No, not good enough. I'll need a new, clean separate plate," says Bo. "It is not by choice, my system can't tolerate poultry drippings."

"I'll get you a clean plate, and clean vegetables," says Jake.

"My system is sensitive, which is a big part of why I am so thin, why my clothes are so baggy," Bo explains. "You know, I know I sound ridiculous, but I really cannot eat certain things without getting sick, really sick. It is easy to make fun of something like that if you don't suffer from it."

"Now that is rough, Bo. No worries," says Jake before speaking with a waiter about bringing a clean plate and, from now on, bowls of separated food dishes.

"I am so, so sorry, man," says Gunth, laying his hand on Bo's shoulder, "I set this meal thing up before we left early this morning, I am never alert when I first wake up. Are you?"

"I think I am too often too alert," answers Bo.

We wake up to a cool morning, and meet for breakfast in an outdoor café. I wear Jake's sweater, socks and gloves. We sit with the English nun we met last night who knows Siri's dad and invites us to do some mountain trekking.

Street cleaners are cleaning the street. A couple wearing facemasks sits at the table next to us. They are camping on a site along the river, and, Jake learns, also attending SACRED FLOW = TRANSFORMATION. Jake asks about the masks, wondering if they are for warmth. "No, for protection," one answers, going on to explain that usually they do not need such protection up here in the mountains away from polluted cities, but street cleaning stirs up enough toxins that their bodies require defense. At this point we lose Jake who sits down to ask them to explain. The rest of us discuss the hiking route we will follow today. We agree to carry fishing gear. The nun pulls out several trail maps. Together we examine them. We agree on a time to meet. She walks to the church across the square. We order more coffee.

"Well I hope Markus comes," I say.

"I doubt at this point he will, Brett," Bo says.

"How do you know his plans?"

"I just do, Brett."

"How do you?" Frances asks.

"I just do. I doubt he will make it," Bo repeats.

Gunth starts taking our pictures. "I've never won an award," he says.

"Bo wins them all of the time," says Frances.

Gunth asks Bo, "How did you choose your life? School, writing, Frances, yoga?"

"Two ways. Gradually and suddenly," answers Bo.

"Gunth, I've seen your photos of me. They turn me into a swan," says Siri, tipping her head back. "My neck is not long and nice, but it looks that way in your shots. How do you do that?"

"Trade secret," Gunth says, snapping another photo.

We take a walk around the town before returning to our rooms. On our way we see the nun outside of the church, planting flowers. She invites us inside. It is a small, spare church and somehow it feels very good as we look at its windows, altar and ceiling; as we sit in its pews.

Things turn warm in the afternoon. The nun provides excellent maps. We hike, then hot and muddy, swim in the river.

We eat our packed lunch: hard rolls, cheese, grapes and sausage, and drink jugs of water, bottled from a nearby spring. Only some of us eat the sausage. We find the spring on one of the nun's maps and plan to head there next, after a little fishing, but we wind up all falling asleep by the bank on top of blankets the hotel provides for us.

Next day Jake takes a day trip to a neighboring village to meet with his good friend, and former colleague, A.E. The two meet several times a year to go fishing and to sort out old times.

The bond between them started when they—young reporters—both worked as scouts at the start of a particularly vicious and unsuccessful occupation. In this case, "scout" describes a member of the press or military, sent out to function as a bridge between citizens and the incoming forces. They sat in on meetings, listening to military strategies for demolishing the enemy, and reported what they learned to the people. Both were there as the war got started, both saw things go far, too far. They saw soldiers and civilians killed instantly, or become slowly, gruesomely mutilated. They saw filthy, makeshift hospital rooms filled with wounded boys writhing on cots or floor blankets, terrorized families, neighborhoods turned into bloodbaths.

I asked Jake once what the worst part of having to view all of this kind of thing again and again was. He rarely responds directly when I ask about his job, but this one time he does answer, "After awhile you get caught between three kinds of bad. Constantly looking at bodies—dead, injured, hurting—knowing you cannot stop the attacks is one. Trying to imagine what goes through someone's mind getting hurt or inflicting the hurt is two. Growing used to seeing and hearing it all is three."

I walk Jake to the bus stop. He carries a pen, notebook. I hand him a paper-wrapped sandwich I asked the hotel staff to prepare for him, and a bottle of water. We hug, kiss, I start to tear up. I do not let him see. Once the bus moves away I feel better, lighter.

When I walk back to the hotel, Siri tells me that Gunth is just back from a visit to the town doctor because of a bad, upset stomach. The doctor suggests a three day fast. Gunth has never fasted before. She jokes that Bo put a spell on him because of the food order mistake. That evening, we sit at a table sipping tea and mineral water. Gunth, who has not eaten all day, behaves uncharacteristically hostile, and directs his bad mood toward Bo.

"Bo, where do you get jollies? Staring at Brett? Listening to Frances belittle you, becoming anorexic. You say, 'My clothes are baggy' like it is a good thing, something to feel proud of."

All of us, including Bo, stare at Gunth, who continues.

"How do you afford getting so many degrees? You must make a lot of money from your books. Unless you have a rich relative. Or relatives. Do you have money, inherited money, hidden money? That would explain your lack of embarrassment about hanging around, never eating. What the fuck, baggy. Baggy, baggy, baggy. Baggy is not necessarily cool. Not necessarily."

I put an arm around Gunth's shoulder. "Calm down Mr. Photographer, your toxins are talking. Bo, it is his toxins, it is not you."

"I don't have as many toxins as you fucking think," says Gunth.

"Ah oh, good thing Jake is not here Gunth," warns Siri.

"What? I'm saying I don't have toxins. It's true."

"Hey," I continue, "Siri means throwing the fuck word at me. And Gunth, you are truly one to talk about hidden money. Where would you be without your family? Come on, show us some of the manners your parents paid a fortune for you to learn."

He nods, "Ok, ok, Brett, sorry, but just let me get this one last point to Bo," he says, laying his hand on Bo's, shoulder, "Just one thing, one fucking favor and I'll stop riding you. Bo, please stop fucking staring at Brett because it makes Frances and Jake embarrassed and me and Siri sick."

When Bo finally speaks it is this: "Jake, embarrassed. Right."

Gunth stares with surprise, "Wow, man. Touché."

They both grin, then start to chuckle, then out and out laugh, exchanging handgrips.

If I am honest, I like to see Gunth hurt Bo; though I also wish he would not do it, because my enjoyment makes me disgusted with myself.

The next night, when Jake gets back and we are alone in our hotel room, I tell him about the incident, and my feelings. He says, "Stop. There is enough real tragedy in this world, your glee in this case is harmless."

"But," I wonder, "isn't my glee part of the problem?"

"If you believe that then you seriously need to get a life. Or at least a different graduate student/psycho-therapist-in-training," Jake says, picking me up, hugging me hard, letting me down beneath him on our room's four-poster bed with crisp white sheets that smell like the clean mountain air outside.

The next morning, Bo approaches me: "Sorry Brett. Sorry I stare at you and annoy you and everybody else around here. Honestly, I wasn't aware. I am glad it was brought to my attention."

"You know, Bo, you should really get yourself checked out, I mean, see if you do have food allergies or intolerances. Maybe if you avoid certain foods you will be able to eat more and eat better."

"Brett," he says, taking my head in his hands and kissing the top of it, "you are an amazingly good-hearted woman."

I do not know what to say, how to answer. It turns out I don't have to say anything because everybody else walks into the lobby at the same time. We all take a walk around the town. At some point, I excuse myself to spend some time alone in our room.

Traveling or not, Jake is always able to find time alone. No one ever questions his departures. I have a very hard time getting off by myself, especially at times like this, traveling with friends. When I am in school I can always have an excuse like I have to study, or I have to write a paper or I have to prepare for a class. But when I am traveling, on a supposed vacation or during supposed leisure time, I do not have those excuses. Of course, Jake does have a job, writing, that requires periods of isolation. Even though the bulk of his work, collecting information by talking to people, seeing where they live, how they live, listening to all the different points of view, requires extensive human contact.

Sometimes I cannot wait to get away and be by myself, but once I am alone I do not know what to do. One thing I do when I travel is to sort through and order things in my luggage, hand washing the silk bras and underpants I always bring with me, because the material feels good next to my skin, and it reminds me I am myself. Sometimes, when traveling, I do not feel like myself, or even remember who that self is. I miss my clothes, my routines, my room and bed. Not all the time, or even every day, just now and then. I do not want to give the impression of complaining, or suggesting that my sort of travel is in any way extreme or even challenging. My friends and I have no real concerns such as: will we find a place to eat, will we find a place to sleep, will we land in a dangerous area, will we run out of friends and money. We certainly do not see anything horrific or tragic the way Jake does when he travels to places, encountering, investigating and reporting on atrocities most of us can barely imagine, no matter how much we read about them. I am trying to talk about how sometimes I just like to get off, by myself, and do small things, not necessarily anything you could describe as interesting or productive.

Just yesterday Frances tells me, "Bo can be so damned helpless and so awful, which makes him my sort of guy."

She relates an anecdote. Once, Bo begged her to let him cut her toenails. After some back and forth she agreed, and he wound up cutting her pinky toe very badly.

Jake has a dark side that can emotionally disturb me and hurt me, yet he would never harm me in a way so physically careless.

Last year, Jake and Frances and Gunth and I sit in a café, drinking beer. Gunth, just back from a trip to the United States, where he photographed boxers in different urban training centers, is in a cheerful, storytelling mood. He tells us about the people who box, their gyms, their training regimes, their neighborhoods. He talks about how Americans are either frightfully fit, or bulky and overweight. He describes how many cities, including my hometown of Detroit, now have casinos. He tells us he made a bundle of money gambling. Bo appears at the café entrance, but instead of joining us he stands still, head bowed. Frances turns toward him.

"Bo, stop looking at your boots," she says.

"Frances," he says, speech slurred, "I am proud of these boots. These are my boots, they are on my feet, I like them. They have covered a lot of ground: pavement, raw earth, studios, beaches, libraries."

"Bo," says Frances, smiling, "I have a present for you." She reaches into her bag and pulls out a pair of sandals, made from recycled rubber.

He sits down next to her, reeking of alcohol, kisses her cheek. Gunth keeps talking about his trip to America and the different kinds of great music he heard there. But it is hard to concentrate because of the tension building between Bo and Frances. Both ignore Gunth. Frances talks quickly, quietly, under her breath. Bo hangs his head, breathes heavily. She talks louder, asks him about a girl, another student. Bo seems to shrink. Frances, on the other hand, blooms. I have never seen her – eyes bright, cheeks flushed, hair shiny – look lovelier. Then, in a voice that is low, even whispery, but loud enough for us at the table to hear, she says, "So, you can go and write about how it happens one more time: you and an undergraduate fuck your brains out and then she falls in love with you and you do your best to let her down easy because you don't have the balls to start up something like that, really. Same old Bo story: You seduce her; she trusts you; you break her heart; you let her down, then scurry away like a little squirrel."

Frances exits the café. Bo, carrying the sandals, follows her. Gunth, Jake and I sit quiet for several minutes.

Markus never does come up to the mountains. We don't see him again until SACRED FLOW = TRANSFORMATION.

5

When we arrive at the conference, SACRED FLOW = TRANSFORMATION, we see people setting up booths to sell yoga props, books, t-shirts, ayurvedic and herbal remedies. There is an organic juice bar. Before long the place seems to explode with people coming in. Friends meeting friends and old lovers, signaling each other by tapping their hearts, making prayer gestures and peace signs, giving each other hugs, exchanging gifts of Eastern deity trinkets and statues. Others, I guess newcomers, stand off to the side wearing gear with logos and holding sticky mats and blankets still in plastic wrap.

Markus, who arrives before us, is there, visible and busy. He wears pale yellow linen Bermudas with a white v-neck t-shirt and a set of orange rubber bracelets. He hugs us all and makes no apology or offers to explain where he has been.

"We have recycling bins, but even so, please limit your use of purchased plastic."

There are product displays, such as an ultra-efficient and tiny cleaning machine I would buy if I owned, instead of rented, a dwelling. I am sure Sigrund, our friend the designer, would buy one for herself and clients. "Littler is Better" is how she describes her design philosophy. Sigrund is happiest with small spatial arrangements. She prefers when rooms and spaces do double duty: dining room/office; library/guest room; kitchen/closet. Of course, she can have a good career that relies upon space moderation in her country, where people are used to small spaces, unlike the vast expanses people are accustomed to in the American Midwest, where I come from.

Siri and I are fascinated by this tiny, powerful washing machine. We watch a young man rub pureed peas, raspberries and brewed coffee onto a shirt, then squirt it with ketchup, before placing it inside the appliance. We stroll around and return to see the shirt displayed, stain-free, in fact blazing white. "Ultrasound waves loosen the dirt and electrolysis cleans the water," explains the demonstrator.

And in addition to product demonstrations, there are mind/body ones.

The first one we see involves watching the teacher/speaker move between challenging physical postures (backbends, arm balances, contorted hand stands) and snippets of ancient philosophy related speech.

"My God he is amazing," says Siri five minutes into it.

"Where my gaze goes determines the position of my spine,"

he says, dropping into a nimble backbend.

"His center of gravity is too low, see how it restricts his movement," whispers Bo.

"A pose need not mean, but be," the speaker says, coming gracefully up. The three of us squeeze one another's hands in acknowledgement.

He does a forward bend, stands up, puts his hands in prayer position, continues.

"People think it is in cities or other populated spaces where futures happen. But it is here, right here," he says, patting his heart with his right hand. "Enlightenment comes from within."

"I guess this is what we have instead of the Bible, church and God," whispers Siri.

Markus and Jake have completely different kinds of charisma. Markus approaches you. Jake stands still, solid, like an oak tree, inviting you to approach, even lean on him.

Markus is a thinker, Jake a reporter. Markus creates, invents ideas and theories, Jake consolidates, articulates, streamlines complex situations.

The first time I ever see Jake, it is in the hospital, scribbling in a pocketsize notebook. He is just back from covering a medical emergency. This particular article, I later learn, contrasts the makeshift tents and sanitation efforts with the facilities of the well-equipped and healthily funded university hospital. I am pretty sure I fell in love with him at that minute, in his Bermudas, long sleeved white oxford, rolled up to his elbows. Brown hair.

Jake has a gigantic appetite. Mine is gigantic too. Ways we sate our appetites differ. He fills his with activities: work, sport, travel. I wish I could fill mine that way, but have not yet developed enough ability. I am stuck on a lower rung: heart, throat, stomach. Talking. Listening. Shopping.

Sometimes it seems that everything interests Jake, or at least is ammunition for his story. "I need to get close to the story, Brett. The more distant you are from your story the more you romanticize it. For me, the reporting itself has to stay clean."

I have waited endlessly for Jake. In churches, cars, stadiums, bars. This is why my yoga practice is so important to me. It teaches me things to do and think about when I wait.

These stories, the daily sorts of ones he encounters with me, are not his hardest work, or the work he feels driven to do. His hard work is done when he is off covering natural or political disasters: wars, droughts, hurricanes and genocides. I read what he writes about these events and barely believe it is him who is writing. I read what he writes and can barely stand imagining how painful experiencing such events, or even being in such settings, must be. He writes so clearly and carefully about what happens to a person, community, town, or country when subjected to terror, frenzy, cruelty and destitution. He writes so clearly about things that start small and snowball into something massive, bad and senseless. His reports capture people's experience. I barely can imagine what these people go through, I force myself to read and learn about it. Jake's reports make this learning possible. But when he returns and I ask him to talk about what he wrote he mostly just stares off into space, eyes paralyzed.

I understand this expression is a form shock. Even though I understand it, the behavior still takes work getting used to.

I say something about his paralysis to Siri, who tells me, "Brett, you know that not everyone can go in different directions. Some people can do one thing, and do not feel responsible if someone with them is cored."

"You mean bored?"

"No, I mean cored, weary, fed up, flayed, down to their core."

The last time I asked Jake about his departures, and the effect they have on him he says, "Brett, I just cannot think through that subject. At one time or another I probably will. I understand my job is damaging to me in some ways, and that it hurts you and I am sorry. But, it is my job. Aside from saying I am sorry, and I am truly sorry because I love you, I do not know where else I can go with that subject."

ooooo

Sometimes, late at night or early in the morning, reading things in a heightened enough mood, I start to believe they actually happened to me or were at least dreams.

6

The first full day of SACRED FLOW = TRANSFORMATION, Jake works in our room. He comes to the conference to finish a long article and spend time with me before his next assignment, rather than to take part in the different offerings. I take a very hot, hard, vinyasa yoga class. That practice is very good. After we eat lunch, Jake, who goes foodless during his marathon work sessions, stays in our room all day without coming out. All he asks is that I bring him a pot of coffee. He works straight through, forgetting about everything else. The rest of us eat rice, vegetables (only steamed and raw are offered during the day) with interesting sauces.

"Couch for you tonight," says Frances to Bo, who sips the vegetable broth, nibbles on chunks of raw carrots, broccoli, and a minced onion, cabbage salad. She adds, "Wind is the enemy for a cabbage consumer's bedmate."

"Shut up Frances," says Bo.

We all are smitten with what the chef, her nametag says Do Rae, does with food. And she is breathtakingly lovely. After lunch, she gives a short talk. Her soft brown hair curls around her ears. She wears one nose ring and four looped earrings on each of her ears.

"My parents named me Do Rae after the famous *Sound of Music* song, 'Do-Ri-Me.' I am Do Rae, my sister is Me Fa." She smiles, and there is a ripple of laughter in the audience. "It was a little embarrassing when I was young, but I think it helped me develop as a chef because I was, supposedly, a musically talented child and having that name turned me away from any interest in music. In the beginning I started off cooking not going by recipes, just making things up, adding different ingredients and seeing how they tasted. But I've moved on. What do I consider when I put together a meal? My guests. This group of you all, for example, is extraordinarily health-conscious. Teenagers, who consume the most amount of food, not counting extreme athletes, don't really care about their food's health qualities. But the thing for me is the feeding. Cooking itself does not interest me as much as feeding people does."

She discusses her menu choices for symposium meals: the rice and spinach balls, the sesame nut torte. She talks about anise seeds, which aid digestion and deter bad breath. She is not at all self-conscious. She speaks of food respectfully, speaks of her cooking as something apart from herself. She starts by saying that sharing meals has, historically, been a foundation for warm human interaction. She goes on to tell us how there are chefs who follow recipes, and those who just cook, how they are two very different things. She says she used to avoid dealing with assertive flavors like tarragon, wild leeks, or even mint, but that now she has learned, through careful balance and experimentation, to use them with confidence.

There is nothing conceited about her. She seems sincerely fascinated by her job, cooking, and sincerely interested in talking about the profession and tasks associated with it. We learn that when she assembles a dish, she not only considers her flavors, but also is equally attentive to color, size, and texture. Her reasons are partly but not purely aesthetic. She talks about eating with your eyes.

"Vary your food colors and your dishes will look pretty but just as important, you are likely to pack in vitamins and minerals." She talks us through examples: broad bands of deep green spinach pasta tossed with feta cheese, toasted pine nuts and roasted red and yellow peppers; spaghetti squash, tomatoes, mushrooms, sugar snap peas. She goes on to say she means mix the colors for a meal of separated foods, not one-dish meals.

She prefers small piles of each color and food type on a plate as opposed to the one mix-up in a big bowl serving.

"There is no friend as loyal as a good dish. And the bottom line about a good dish is you can feed people. Feeding people makes them and me happy."

At the end of Do Rae's talk Markus says, "Nobody ever lives their life all the way up except a good chef and she is that."

Evening. Jake walks out of our room, erect and bleary eyed. Takes my head in his hands, kisses my forehead. "Finished."

I hand him an apple.

Who can do that for a whole day? Stay in a room, not eat, work. Even finish. Have I mentioned we are in a stunning geographic setting, and the weather is warm in the day, cool in the evenings. In other words, perfect. See this example of Jake's discipline, determination and willpower.

He emerges from our room wanting food and movement. We decide to take a walk and then eat. On our way out, Jake chews the apple. We pass through the gymnasium/conference room. It is filling up with even more travelers; standing all huddled along the walls and lined up for registration tickets. They fought weekend traffic to get here. Another line of people waits in front of the registration desk. Some stand or sit on luggage, others squat on the ground, with their blankets and yoga props: bolsters, blocks, mat duffel-carriers around them. The moon is just coming out.

Markus approaches, gives us each a bear hug, says, "Have you listened to these people talking about their diets, bowel movements, nostril cleansing routines, debating the wisdom of practicing yoga this evening, because of the moon being full? I thought that kind of talk only happened in the U.S. of A."

"This reminds me," says Jake, "of the time I went to a bullfight. People waiting with newspapers to buy tickets."

"But not talking so candidly about bodily functions, surely, or even lunar cycles."

"You know," Jake continues, "wind is the bullfighter's greatest enemy."

"Frances said something like that to Bo at lunch today," I say.

"I bet she did," Jake says.

"So," Markus turns to me, "how do you like the conference?"

"Fine," I say. Jake grips his apple, looks around, taking in the scene.

Markus continues, "Frankly I am uncomfortable. These functions have their place, I mean, don't we all want to avoid the boredom and despair of a material world? But, honestly, it is presumptuous to believe we can figure out how. We cannot. We are human. Tedium and despair are integral to our condition."

"You think?" asks Jake.

"I don't mean our condition is defined by these things, but they come with the challenge of being human; we cannot and should not try to eradicate them. It is pretty ballsy for a person to say he or she has the potential to reach divinity."

"There sure seem to be a lot of rules at these functions. I heard a term the other day, 'spiritual correctness,'" says Jake.

Markus nods his head, "Precisely what I am talking a about. As if following certain rules can lead one to spirituality."

"Spiritual correctness sets a tone."

"Or those rules could be like a recipe?" I interject.

"I bet most people attending this conference avoid meat, coffee, alcohol and don't let themselves express anger, or try not to express it. But are they better, happier, closer to things spiritual than people who blow their top once in awhile and have a hotdog and coke or beer for lunch?"

Jake says, "I thought spirituality was not supposed to be judgmental."

Markus says, "Exactly, see, you understand me. Everyone acknowledges things are missing but then they believe what is missing can be found. I am not sure that is the way to go about it. Imperfect humans, imperfect world. Why not stress our imperfections, even celebrate them? Denial of what makes us human creates false personas. I should know, I am a part of this problem." Pause. Then, "Jake Barnes, I deeply admire your intellect."

"I'm no intellectual," answers Jake.

"Americans always say that," says Markus.

"Not true," says Jake, "at least if you count Mark Twain as an American. He said something about intellectual 'work' being misnamed because it is a pleasure, a high reward. He said something like that."

"Well," says Markus, "because you know that quote, I would say you are at least partly in the intellectual camp, like it or not."

He puts his finger to his lips, a signal for quiet, and tilts his palm, shows us an audio-recorder, records a couple walking by.

"Listen," says Markus, playing what he just recorded:

"I hate to think of the germs traveling through a yoga room, between the floor and the air, with all those people's bare feet, heavy breathing and sweat. Don't we just absorb everyone else's toxins?"

"Let me tell you," says Markus, "there are people here who are deceptively civilized."

"They can be self-righteous," says Jake.

"To put it mildly."

"Self-centered, too."

"Bingo. We are back to being judgmental again. They really can be dangerous when they are all together in a group. Separate, they are diffused."

"Markus," says Jake, "People are always more broadminded when you talk to them individually and more conservative, more judgmental, in a group."

"Jake, always so fair," I say.

"It is true, believe me," he answers.

Two other people walk by. Markus holds out his recorder.

"What is the conference like?"

"Good, pretty good. Too early to tell. And my judgment is always off on a moon day."

Markus widens his eyes.

"Is this a data collection strategy, and is it legal?" asks Jake.

"Yes to both questions," answers Markus. "Here, listen to what I accidentally taped between Bo and Frances when we were out walking earlier today." He clicks his recorder:

"That clinic performs wonderful colonics. And I should know," says Bo.

"Shut up Bo," says Frances.

Markus clicks the recorder off.

"Did you know he is getting colonics too? I mean, I am worried," Markus says.

"Consider him as going through a phase. And listen, seriously, he could have some severe food allergies or intolerances. I think you should encourage him to get that checked out," I say.

"Point well taken, Brett."

Jake and I leave Markus, walk around the town, find a café and sit at a table outside, discuss whether guerilla recording is or may some day be subject to legal regulation.

Jake and I order wine, soup, and grilled fish. He cups my chin in his hand, "I am uninterested in whether or not Bo gets colonics, how about you?"

When we've finished eating we see Do Rae at a neighboring table, knitting. I explain who she is to Jake and invite her to sit at our table. I had not had a chance to tell Jake about her. It turns out Jake knows her parents. "I remember that name," Jake says. Then, "I was reading something about chefs' worries about toxins; are you worried about food poisoning?"

"Always," she laughs, and stops knitting for a moment. "But I can't tell anyone. Only a very bad chef, or a paranoid one, would talk about that. You never know about ingredients; you never know how much bacteria an ingredient might have these days. Maybe that is why I love cooking with cabbage. It is versatile and very cleansing. Why shouldn't a chef worry, isn't concern a good, good thing?"

"Concern, good, yes," says Jake. "Worry, probably no. We think our friend Gunth might have gotten some food poisoning, but not here."

"Do you know there was food poisoning at last year's symposium? They traced it to the raw produce in the organic juice bar," Do Rae says.

"Was anyone seriously hurt?"

She shakes her head, no.

Bo approaches our table with raw juice drinks in his hand.

"Would you introduce me to your friend" he asks Jake and me.

Do Rae looks up from her piece of knitting. It goes well with her small, thick, well-formed fingers, and the color of the yarn — forest green — suits her face. We introduce them.

"You, it is you who cooked that wonderful meal. Very pleased to meet you. And now what are you doing with your hands?" Bo asks, sitting down.

"Well, making these scarves has turned into a hobby. There is something really satisfying about it, like cooking. I start, then finish."

Bo says, "I understand the task completion parallel, but the food is consumed, don't tell me even your scarves are edible."

"No, no but I have a rule; I give all my scarves away. What would I do with all of them, hanging around?"

"Well then," Bo leans toward her, "Can I have one? Can Jake, can Brett?"

"Well," she blushes, head down.

"I'm sorry, that must have sounded pushy."

"Well, uhm," she continues, raising her head, looking him in the eye, "Do you like scarves?"

"Then, now and always," he says, reaching a long index finger to his neck, rubbing an insect bite. "Scarves are protective, and I am thin-skinned."

She watches him. She has a triangular scar on her chin. Her sturdy hands and tan arms show scars from cooking burns.

She takes a tin from her pocket. "Would you like to taste these pretty anise seeds?"

"You like anise seeds?" he asks.

"Oh yes, I often use anise, it is good for your breath." She smiles.

Jake and I accept a small pile of seeds, leave to take a walk around the city. We stand on a hill, overlooking a wild landscape, hold each other tightly. The full moon makes everything visible. I realize my sweater and water bottle are at the table. When we return, Bo and Do Rae are gone but the anise seeds had spilled. A young man in an apron comes with a cloth and wipes them off.

7

The next day, Jake and I sit at a table playing checkers. Do Rae is across the room at a table with some of the kitchen staff. Bo approaches.

"Brett, Jake, I gotta tell you, I'm a goner. I'm mad about that chef. I need her. I need Frances too, but that Do Rae, I can't stop my feelings for her. Feel, feel my hands." We each take one, and they are ice-cold, pale, thin and shaking.

"What must you all think of my excessive regulation: yoga, degrees, food, my book; and my interests, you, Brett, and now this chef. Do you think my interest in Do Rae comes from a bad or a good place? Admit it, eating food made by a cook like that on a regular basis, you could figure out how never to get sick. And another thing, you could eat her foods all day and never gain an ounce. And fuck Frances with her comments on wind breaking, wind is a friend to your body; bodily emissions are healthy. She eats meat and drinks coffee all day and doesn't smell so great herself. Brett, Jake, tell me honestly: Do you think I've really lost my way, my direction? I just cannot fast and nostril cleanse and get degrees and organize conferences and write books and practice yoga all the time."

"There she is, at a table with her prep cooks," I say.

"I'll wave her over," suggests Jake.

"Oh she might not come if she sees me," says Bo.

"Bo," I say, "she'll come over. Really she will."

"I've always done what I want. Now maybe I can be there for someone, help someone else blossom," he says.

Jake waves his hand and smiles at the table of kitchen staff.

Do Rae approaches with a plate of small appetizers. "Seaweed, fennel, peas, mint, chard," she says, pointing to different beautiful green concoctions, rolled up.

"You must eat some of these appetizers with me. I am having a green moment," she says, setting the plate down, sitting down herself. She has very nice manners. Through the window, we see Frances and Gunth and Siri across the street. They wave and point to an apothecary they are going into.

Do Rae is polite to Jake and I, but really focused on Bo. She had seen him with Frances, understands there is something between them and wants to be careful not to offend.

"Do you cook every day?" I ask.

"Oh yes," she answers.

She and Bo's hands touch when they reach for the chard appetizer at the same time. She takes his hand. "I also read fortunes," she says.

"Oh no," says Bo, "Don't look into my soul yet. I have much, much to hide. My aggression leads me to a very bad place."

"Yes," she smiles, "I can see."

He shifts into the lotus position on the chair.

"But," she laughs, "I can tell from this pressure point in the hand: you have a good liver."

She puts herself in the exact same lotus position, except reversed, as Bo.

The rest of the group come out of the apothecary and pass by, telling us they are going to an emotion management seminar before the party that evening. Jake and I leave Bo and Do Rae and walk with our friends.

"Don't look at me like that; it is fine, they are fine, he needs to discuss food with someone," Frances says, taking out a small pretty compact, putting on fresh lipstick.

That evening we reassemble for a next to the last night party. Tables of juice, bottled waters; organic beers and wines; bowls of rice and pumpkin; kale and broccoli; plates of carrot and fig cakes. People have changed into festive skirts of yellow, blue, pink stripes trimmed with gold braid, fine shirts stitched with red silk and embroidered with little silver flowers, and silver-embroidered belts. Siri and I both wear black dresses. Some people go barefoot, others wear sandals, clogs; a few even wear boots with heels. A harmonious and non-violent atmosphere. Siri points out Gunth with a plate of steamed rice in front of him. "Now he is eating. Hopefully food will put an end to the nastiness."

We see Bo deep in conversation with Do Rae. He seems to give a short sob; she puts her hand on his shoulder. "You know our Bo," says Frances, "always having to broad-band his suffering. He sure knows how to get the girl."

"Don't be upset, Frances," says Siri.

"I am not upset. But I might throw up," she answers.

At some point in the evening we notice that Bo and Do Rae are gone.

Not long after, one of the older chefs approaches us. "Do Rae is young and inexperienced, she should not mix with your group."

"I'd say you are right, but how to stop her?" asks Jake.

That whole night is like parties before finals week at college. People dance, kiss, eat, drink, but all in a mood trying to ignore tension.

8

Next morning. I go to a long early yoga practice. No one else from our group is there. During it I sweat excessively, losing the sickened sense I've felt creeping up on me. Lying in shavasana I feel relieved, even happy. We are a privileged group. We are young, know very little, expect a whole lot. But It seems like we are well-intentioned people after all, flawed but essentially nice, even loving. I come back to our room, take a shower, wake up Jake. We spend the morning in bed, rent a car to drive out in the country, away from the conference in the afternoon. It is a hard day, but very good. Seeing his friend A.E. up in the mountains was rough on Jake. A.E. has had a difficult time functioning since his position as a scout. And I know Jake spent yesterday writing about it, and that that makes him low. I do not ask about his upcoming assignment. I hope he will tell me, since it starts soon.

Later, at night, we walk by the conference complex. Different parties are in full force. Seminars continue. Music plays. It is a chaotic, festive scene.

Outside one of the seminar buildings we see and greet our friends.

"We've been thrown out," says Frances, laughing, "for lapping milk product."

"Meow," says Markus.

"No. We were ousted because of the turkey drumstick Gunth took out and started gnawing on like a medieval knight," says Siri.

"It was a piece of beef jerky," says Gunth.

"Worse, meat. Red meat. And at this sort of event. Inexcusably bad form," says Siri.

"Hey," says Gunth, "I don't partake in the form, I just photograph."

"Fasting made you weird," says Siri.

"But I'm eating again," says Gunth.

Jake says, "You can't all be thrown out of the whole symposium?"

"No, just the spirituality and capitalism seminar," answers Frances.

"Well, those folks cannot occupy the whole symposium," says Jake.

"They criticize Markus, yet they completely misunderstand Markus," says Frances.

"Let's go back in," suggests Siri. "Markus, you deserve a chance to explain yourself."

"No Siri," says Frances, "Markus does not need to sink to their level. Those people in there don't make points, they set a tone. An extremely judgmental tone. And not one of them convinced me they understood his position, his methods, truly. Jump all over him before they comprehend."

"I've kept Frances out of plenty of fights tonight," says Markus, "She's on a roll." Then to Frances, "Come on, it is just a seminar. You could teach them a thing or two about reverence and a free market."

"Good old Frances," says Gunth.

Frances says, "They can't insult Markus, I won't stand for it."

"So there was something more than Gunth's jerky," Jake says.

Frances's voice breaks, "Damn their picky judgmental non-specific tone, spoiling the spirit of our symposium."

"Hey," says Markus, flashing a set of very white teeth, "I don't care. Their loss. Do you even care?"

"No," says Gunth, putting an arm around Jake's shoulder.

"I wish I were depleted," says Frances.

"They insulted Markus?" Jake asks.

"I wish I were depleted," says Frances.

"Well, in a general tone sort of way," says Gunth.

"I wish I were depleted," repeats Frances. "Then I'd have a good excuse."

We all stop talking and look at one another.

"Then," she continues, "I'd have an excuse. An excuse for why Bo is leaving me."

Her face grows red, "Who cares," she says, "I don't care. Gunth does not care, Jake does not care, Brett and Siri do not care, do you all the fuck care?"

"Yes," Jake says, "I care."

"Me too," say Siri and I at the same time.

Markus puts an arm around Frances's shoulder, "Are you depleted, drained?"

"Of course I am," she collapses. "You don't care, do you Gunth?"

"Me, I take pictures," he answers.

"You cold asshole, Gunth," says Siri.

Markus says, "I wish to hell I were depleted. Then I would not have to travel so goddamn much. Maybe if I were depleted I'd be able to relax, spend quality time with my family. See the limitations and strengths of my methodologies more objectively."

"Those people inside the seminar are just self-absorbed," Gunth says. "We'll look later at my photos and I'll show you that. It does not matter what self-absorbed people say."

"Now that is absurd, even to me," says Markus. "Who is not self-absorbed? Do you think we are not self-absorbed?"

Frances continues, "I'm going to pollute them, slip some veal stock into their vegan soup. Bo's too."

"Bo would notice," says Siri, "he can detect the smell."

"They should not have kicked out a fun group like you," says Jake.

Gunth asks Frances, "Do you know them?"

Frances, wiping her nose, answers, "No. I never saw them in my life. Maybe they saw me with Bo. They said they knew me."

Siri says, "Don't worry, if we run into them again I won't let them say nasty things."

"Come on," says Jake, "Let's go walk."

Gunth, next to Siri, says, "You knew them. Were those your friends?"

Siri answers, "Yes I knew them. They were my friends. Are not now. Zeros, all zeros."

"One of them is a girl from Ann Arbor," says Gunth.

"I was never in Ann Arbor," says Frances.

"I was in Ann Arbor, for years," says Siri.

"I want to get de-plet-ed," sings Markus as we reach the hotel. He puts an arm around Frances, says, "As far as this Bo thing goes, listen, maybe you'll be better off. What is meant to be usually is."

Markus sees students in the lobby sipping the herbal tea the management leaves out for guests, he takes Frances's arm and the two walk over toward them.

Jake whispers to Gunth, "So, what went on in there?"

Gunth answers, "Some one called Markus a hypocrite for having a family and being on the road so much. Then they saw

Gunth chewing beef jerky." Pause. "And a young woman threw a drink at Frances. Said Frances had slept with her boyfriend."

"Now the real story," says Jake.

I say, "Frances is handling this Bo thing so well."

Jake looks at me, "Do you know Frances lies?"

"No, no I...what do you mean?"

"She sleeps with a lot of people, while they are still attached to their lovers and husbands. But says she does not."

"No," I say, "she does not." Then, "I did not know this."

I think to myself, for no reason I understand, that this makes her a more desirable and powerful person than I had thought.

I say, "Siri, did you know this, Gunth, did you?"

Siri says, "I had my suspicions."

Gunth says, "I've taken photos, never shown anyone though. Her business. Has to be tough, being with Bo so much."

Jake says, "Not everyone is as benevolent as you are toward her. I can tell you without even having been in there that those girls in there were mad at Frances because she slept with their boyfriends. That is usually what girls get mad about."

Siri sighs, "But why not get mad at the guys. See this gender thing?"

Bo approaches us, panting, "Where is Do Rae?"

"I don't know," we answer.

Gunth says, "I thought she was with you."

Siri says, "She must have gone to bed."

Bo curls his lip, says, "No, she is not there. She is not in her bedroom."

"Well, I don't know where she is," says Siri.

Frances and Markus return to us.

"Do you know where Do Rae is?"

"Bo you are a clod but you have major nerve," says Frances.

Bo, his face looking yellow in the night, "One of you knows where she is, you know."

"Well, I do not know," I say.

He stands up, "Tell me where she is. You know, you all know."

Jake, "Sit down. I don't know where she is and I don't think Frances or Gunth or Brett or Siri or Markus do either."

Bo says, "The hell they don't."

Gunth snaps, "Bo, shut your anorexic face."

Bo puts his face close to Gunth's, says, "Tell me where she is."

Gunth, "I'm not telling you a damn thing."

Bo responds, "You know where she is."

Jake says, "Bo, you are way out of line."

Gunth moves away from Bo, says, "Why don't you leave. So I don't have to document how ugly your face looks right now."

"Fuck yourself," says Bo.

Frances steps in, says, "Hey Bo, she is off with one of the yoga teachers, on a honeymoon, the fucking kind, is that what you want to hear?"

"Is it true?" Bo says. "It is true, you all know this and are laughing at me." He sits down on the ground, crumbles into a sob.

We all stand together, quietly. Then, Frances crouches down, puts her arm around his shoulder. He immediately embraces her. The two rock back and forth in each other's arms.

"Frances, I am sorry, I am so so so sorry," says Bo.

"Don't. Let's not talk about it Bo. Let's never, ever talk about it," Frances says gently.

"Frances, I try to get away from you but it is with you, only with you, I am able to see things."

"Come on Bo, I am going to put you in a hot, scented bath."

"Frances, do you know that in about thirty-five years we'll be dead?"

"What the hell, Bo," Frances says. "What the hell."

They stand and walk out of the lobby toward their room.

Next morning, our final morning, we sit together in a coffee shop, down the street from the conference center. The conference ended last night and we are going off in our different directions. Some of us head back to school, Markus flies to the United States to be with his family and teach for a semester. Jake travels to report on a region whose deep-seated political and social turmoil are bubbling over, and starting to generate widespread unrest.

Markus comments that the goal of this conference, and of his entire body of work, is to point out that we, each of us, will be all right, as long as we have a passion. And for those of us who do not have a passion yet, it is fine if we connect to another person's passion. Sometimes connecting to a passion, even the passion of someone else, helps you develop your own.

Jake and I walk to our room to pick up our luggage and to share a moment before saying goodbye.

"Jake, I am so sad you are leaving."

"Brett, I love you more than I have ever loved any woman,

and I am sure I love you more than I ever will love any woman. I want to be together with you, always."

"Will it always be like this, you traveling to dangerous situations, reporting on them? Will you always do that?"

"Brett, please, do not make it seem as if it is a choice. Between things. My job and you, for example. That is plain unfair."

"I know," I say, tearing up, burying my head in his neck, "I know." We stay that way for a while. I raise my head, ask him something I have been wondering about.

"Jake, will you be gone for a long time?"

He takes my head in his hands, kisses my forehead, answers, "Brett, I shouldn't be, there won't be a war. I do not feel one coming, so I do not think I will be gone for long. I should see you in a few weeks. But I should be careful. It is a nasty habit I have sometimes, having a strong hunch and expecting to be right."

2
BRY

...learned it painfully and thoroughly
ERNEST HEMINGWAY

So... *Harvest* is my first writing experience of inventing, not simply documenting. The favorite novel from my past, you might already know, that I model it after is, *The Sun Also Rises*, by Ernest Hemingway. There are so many books I love, why does this one particularly hold my attention, draw me in, make me want to interact.

Hemingway's characters live completely different lives than I do. They have time on their hands, freedom. They can lack direction, search for things to do, think, feel, be; they can interact dramatically. They are not tied to a home or routine; no one bathes or feeds children, works a day job, cooks dinner, does laundry, vacuums, oversees schooling. Their free time allows for the thrill, the romance, of travel, and of viewing a bullfight.

His original title for the novel was *Fiesta*.

Hemingway ends his novel with a question: "Isn't it pretty to think so?" Here is what leads up to it:

"Oh Jake," Brett said, "we could have had such a damned good time together."

Ahead was a mounted policeman in khaki directing traffic. He raised his baton. The car slowed suddenly pressing Brett against me.

"Yes," I said, "Isn't it pretty to think so?"

What a sad, punishing little line. But that is Hemingway packing so much into just a few words.

The question refers, in part, to the impossibility of Jake Barnes and Lady Brett Ashley ever having their version of a full-blown, long-term, love affair. That Jake, Hemingway's, was physically injured in the war. My Jake has emotional wounds, also from combat. Sometimes it is tricky to know which is the harder kind of injury to handle, long-term. Hemingway's Jake is a soldier; mine is a war reporter. I think Hemingway's question also refers to the fact that his bright, privileged young characters traveling through Europe, drinking in Paris, attending bullfights in Spain (drinking there too) are not guaranteed the golden futures they believed they would have.

Anyway, my last line (Jake, "It is a nasty habit I have sometimes, having a strong hunch and expecting to be right.") tries to capture something similar to and different from Hemingway's. My line puts across a downward shift; a move from being certain to uncertain. I understand if someone thinks that *Harvest* is not actually inventive writing, since it is so closely modeled after Hemingway's magnificent novel. I might even agree, I do not know. Because the point of writing *Harvest* is not to create something good, it is to give me something to think about. Having written it makes me more comfortable around people who are consistently thinking about and doing interesting and creative things like our older twins, my husband Euge, Bitty, my father-in-law, and the Assistant.

The truth is, none of them (except the older twins) even know about *Harvest*'s existence.

Hemingway's Lady Brett seemed not to have a real profession. My Brett practices yoga and studies psychology. She has a potential for passion (and a career) that, I think, makes her less dependent on other people to entertain her. Plus, she narrates the story. This is another way she is engaged. The glamorous, charismatic Lady Brett, on the other hand, relies on entertaining others, or depends on others to entertain her. And when she is bored with one person she moves on to the next. Not my Brett, though.

Working closely with Ernest Hemingway, his very good brain with its language and storytelling skills, gives me a singular sort of stimulation. So maybe the point of me writing those eighty or so pages, is to give me someone and something to connect to; to think about. Hemingway wrote, hands down, a great story and he put the whole thing together beautifully. I do not know if he wrote it to have something to think about. I do not know how he felt about the characters during and then after writing his book. My story is not nearly as great, and certainly not as well put together, but writing it did make me a more interested, involved-with-the-world person.

   I wish I could view raising our young twins as interesting. I truly, truly do. Raising them gives me a lot to do but not a lot to think about. I love my children but I am not always interested in them. And I do not like the interesting things I think about to come only from the people who make up my close friends and family. Or what I see in the theater or on the streets or read in books. That position makes me feel, to use an expression from a line in the play Bitty currently appears in, deadbeat. Who wants to be around a deadbeat? Sure, people see how healthy and happy our twins are and respect me for taking such good care of them in this new city with my husband working so hard. But I do not want to just be a good caretaker.

   I want to have things to do and things to think about.

   This can be tricky when you live somewhere, like I do, that is interesting, stimulating. Living in a city like this, packed with out of the ordinary persons and things, it is easy to feel drab by comparison, to feel left out. Or to be so overwhelmed by it all you get sidetracked, lose focus. This city offers so much to take in, to do, but it is hard, for me anyway, to take time to sit and think. Reflect. Like the song "Moon River" asserts, there's such a lot of world to see. But if you spend all of your time seeing there is never time to do anything, create, articulate, put something down. Seeing turns into a kind of consuming. When do you stop taking things in, let them settle, breathe, and send them out?

Interesting, interested people, I believe, are invested in a social contract. Not just their neighborhood, close friends and family. But invested in things out, beyond. Things that include them, but extend out, beyond. The thing is it is not always possible to leave that circle, to mingle with those outside of it. For me personally, I mean.

Anyway, now I realize these different reasons help explain why I write, and feel comforted by *Harvest*. The experience reminds me of spending time with toys in my childhood bedroom, particularly with my large dollhouse, which was built and given to me by my grandmother. The three-story structure with an attic, multiple rooms, indoor and outdoor furniture. Surrounding the house itself was a lawn with a swing set and a little pond. I had different dolls living there. Grandmother did not make the dolls, but she scaled the house to insure that the dolls built by Dr. George fit into that house. Dr. George, a good family friend (and, turns out, Grandmother's special friend), was our town eye doctor. In his spare time, when not seeing patients, testing their vision, fitting them for glasses, or hanging out with Grandmother, he made dolls. I spent a lot of time with those dolls, my dolls, the ones he made, and with their house, its grounds and furniture, making up a world, making up friends. I mean, friends, real ones, would visit and play with us too, I am not saying I only played alone with personalities I invented. I am saying, remembering, how inventing personalities and interacting with them in the form of dolls was a big part of my childhood. Beth, the brown haired ballerina; Leslie, the blond bookworm. Charlie, the stocky, dirty boy, who broke things and spied.

With *Harvest* I again have the chance to create and play with characters. I make new friends with those personalities, invented by Ernest and me, together. I believe in, connect to, and love them.

When I finish the project I feel loss. Sure, I enjoy my actual friends and family. And children. But something about the characters in *Harvest* is different and I miss them.

Because: I do. Love. Them.

I love, and miss imagining, the make-up sex between Bo and Frances, all of the sex between Jake and Brett, Do Rae's food, the mountainous landscape, Markus Duker's laid-back elegance.

There are times Euge is out of town or busy working. The grown-up twins are off doing their midnight theater rehearsals. Bitty performs on stage, Jorje and the Assistant work late in a marathon session the way fashion designers must do. They have a crew of help. Before a show, they spend most of their time with that crew, since things come down to the wire. At these times it is the little twins and I. No adult company. These are not satisfying times for me, in general. It is when I do a great deal of support work: clean, shop, cook, wash, iron. Organize schedules, oversee schoolwork, make sure shoes still fit. Speak with other parents. I sometimes get very lonely doing all of this "parenting."

I know some parents, especially with busy spouses, rely on each other during busy, lonely child-caring times. They connect with people in their neighborhood or those they have met at the school of their children to help them through. They talk on the phone or swap hand-me-downs. Then there are parents who are very busy with their jobs, personal travel, fundraising activities, volunteering on museum and symphony boards, and have full-time nannies. They never get bogged down in day-to-day childcare. Not to say they are uninvolved with their children, just to say the involvement does not bog them down.

For the record: I do not know what makes a good parent (I used to know, or think I did, back when I ran a pre-school, before I gave birth to my own twins), but I doubt it has to do with the amount of time you spend with your children. I think it has to do with your personality. Some personalities love spending time with their children. They enjoy parks, picture books, birthday parties, lessons, circle games, arts and crafts projects, nap-times. They do not mind reprimanding, rule enforcing, consoling, breaking up fights, cleaning up tomato sauce ground into the carpet, wiping noses, saying, "No" to the high-pitched tune of the ice cream truck – firmly, not angrily – and removing children from a scene when they begin to wail and throw a tantrum.

Others would rather be, or have to be, busy with their own projects during the day and enjoy special time with their kids later. Walk the dog, eat dinner, fold laundry. Take kids shopping, to dance and music lessons, films, to the planetarium. Watch television, play catch or board games. Hang out.

In general, you tend not to encounter parents with full-time help at the grocery store or in the park. You might see them eating out somewhere, or attending a film, play or concert. You probably will find them as spectators at their kids' sports games, play rehearsals, recitals.

Of course I emphasize *in general*. I do not mean to suggest this is always the way things are all of the time. I am just relating my version of things; what I see in my life here, in this city.

I have not connected very well with any parent here, in this big city.

I go to morning coffees, even sometimes walk in the park afterward. I volunteer on committees and I sometimes go to Parent Happy Hour. But in truth, these things make me feel lonely. The parents here, or at our kids' school anyway, are serious, competitively serious. There are so many different areas of rivalry. Professional rivalry is huge. But hobby engagement (style, golf, religious devotion, choral singing, cooking, knitting, fitness routines and levels, book clubs) is equally cutthroat.

I used to pride myself in thinking the best of others. Now, since finishing *Harvest,* I am not so sure I still do. This is something that really bothers me. When I ran the pre-school back home, and even here, while working on *Harvest,* I was a less judgmental person. At the pre-school, I dealt with parents and children. But I was so busy working: teaching, structuring, talking, intervening, listening, training, I rarely had time to judge. It just was not a part of my thought process.

I truly was a different person then. I can barely remember that person now.

Bitty gets irritated with me when I express this to her. She thinks I exaggerate and am also being whiney, even self-aggrandizing. She says I should be careful about making it seem as if I am better than all of these other mothers, by overstating, and over-simplifying, their use of time; overall strengths and weaknesses; their child care; their income bracket; their hobbies. She thinks I should be more sympathetic about their drive, and what happens to drive when you give birth to and raise children. She says I have too much time on my hands and I have been overly critical of others lately (so far she knows nothing about *Harvest,* the writing or the completing of it). On the one hand, she is right. Since finishing *Harvest* I have been less accepting of others. But on the other had, Bitty makes interaction sound so easy. Let her try parenting in this city, in our neighborhood. Let her raise our children, and interact with others raising theirs.

She sees some of what happens when I spend concentrated time with a group of mothers from school. These women, physically fit (safe to say excessively so) display an ambition that initially impresses me. My involvement with them temporarily engages me, distracts me from the loss of Harvest. But it does not work for long.

Here is what happens. One morning, a mom, pretty, dressed in a sweat suit, sneakers, approaches me at morning drop-off. She tells me I look fit and wonders if I exercise. I tell her we have a swimming pool on our roof and, in warm weather, I sometimes swim there. But otherwise, no, not really. She tells me she and a group of mothers go to a nearby gym every morning to triathlon train, and invites me to join them. Maybe tomorrow?

She points to the group. There they stand. Oh, I think, those women. I have, honestly, noticed them, admired them, felt dwarfed by them. They are not the professional moms, carefully dressed, with no time to linger. Not the tired-looking moms carrying chewed-up sippy cups, wearing sweat suits that they might have slept in, with strands of dog hair on the seat, huddling together, complaining about how dirty their kitchens are, how much weight they have put on. Not the moms in tunics and flip-flops, dreamily heading off to yoga or meditation. No. These moms wear ponytails under sport caps, tinted moisturizer, clear lip-gloss, and seem to be (like the professional moms) in a hurry, or at least revved up.

These women are fast moving and take their triathlon training seriously, as seriously as a job. The event preparation, I learn, means hours of running, biking, swimming, weight lifting, yoga (the hard core, fast paced, vinyasa kind, not the slow, stretching kind). I join them, and for a while forget about missing *Harvest*. In fact, the intense training causes me to reach moments of incredible highs, running outside along the river, swimming, spinning (in a class, with music blaring), doing push-ups in yoga class, back bending, all leading up to give me bulges of muscle where loose skin once was. I cannot say I enjoy the training, but its rigor distracts me. It gives me something to do, or enough to do that I can stop thinking about, stop missing, stop grieving the completion of *Harvest*. And it also makes me stop thinking about my past, which I had been thinking about constantly, ever since the twins started pre-school. I think especially of my favorite doll, and constant friend, Karen.

My dollhouse, its dolls and furniture never leave my bedroom; they are not meant for transport. But Karen, long hair, chubby, sweet, dimpled cheeks, wide eyes, is transportable; she comes on errands I do with Mom, to all my play dates, to the park sandbox and swing-set. I talk with her, whisper secrets, make a place for her next to me in bed. Then one day, walking home from the school park, she is gone. I run back to the park and cannot find her. Not on the swings, not on the merry-go-round, not on the slide. Not in the sandbox. Not on any park grass or dirt. I start to cry. I ask my mother, "Where is Karen? Where is she?"

"Dead," my mother answers.

I gasp, and begin to cry.

"Honey," Mother continues, "everyone and everything dies at some time. Karen is in heaven and very happy so you do not have to worry."

My mother does not understand. I feel very, very, badly about losing Karen. Awful. I have never, at this point in my life, felt so awful. But, I want to tell my mom: missing Karen is not the same thing as worrying about her. I miss her. I am not worried about her. I want to hold her against my chest, talk with and dress her, brush her hair. I do not feel better knowing she is in a good place like heaven.

But I do not tell my mother this because it sounds mean and selfish.

This is how I feel when I complete *Harvest;* I do not care what happens to it, I just care that it is gone. I miss and want it. I want that world, want it back, or at least be able to visit it. I want to travel with Jake, Brett, Markus, Siri, Gunth, Do Rae, Frances, and even Bo. I want to go to the convention and drive through mountains, I want to practice yoga with them, to eat the food and drink the wine they consume. I want to be in love with a man like Jake, who attributes his intimacy problems to an important job: covering global tragedy. I love him and now he is gone. We, Ernest and I, just make him and everyone else up; I love them all and now they are gone. And I do not even have Ernest to turn to. It is not as if he is even alive anyway. I could have at least picked a living author to make something with. A living author whose book I could rewrite, then maybe I could at least hope to some day meet him or her. But I choose someone long dead. This whole loss makes me very sad. So the period of triathlon training blots all that out.

    This is probably the difference between a real writer and me. A real writer is probably concerned with the quality of his or her body of work, the oeuvre, and once one story is finished, another one starts. I, in contrast, just want to move to a different world when my own feels boring. Triathlon training works for a while, but very soon makes me boring. I become one fit bore. All I do besides parenting is eat and exercise. And these triathlon-training moms turn out to be seriously big gossips. I thought their physical exertion might replace the need to speak badly about others. But they really gossip: that woman's husband does drugs; that child needs extra tutoring; that mom is bulimic; that family's house is a mess; that couple has had plastic surgery; that family lost a child and never told their older children; those two moms are having an affair; that mom with the older husband is in major debt.

    What am I supposed to do with this information? It makes me very uneasy. Having all of this knowledge is a big responsibility, and I already have heavy-duty responsibility with my own life and family. All of this extra knowledge (some meant to be secret) and the liability it brings is way too much extra stuff for me to handle.

Euge comes home with interesting stories about his clients at the gym, the fishing, the river, the rock climbing. I just listen. I do not tell him about the gossip. I do cut myself a second slice of cake and fill him in on the kids and how sore I am. This is one thing about triathlon training: you can eat and eat, almost as much as when nursing twins. But after awhile, eating that much food, runner's high and sore muscles are not so rewarding. So I quit, or, to use the word Euge suggests, stop. He says, "You do not quit you stop. Stop does not carry the negative connotation, honey, and you've done nothing to feel bad about."

When I stop my triathlon training, things became socially unpleasant. First my ex-fellow trainees ignore me, then they express active dislike.

I tell Bitty how not one of them talks to me anymore at school drop-off or pick-up. I tell her I see one in the grocery store who turns her back and walks in the other direction. How I see one on the street who burrows into her cell phone.

Bitty listens, and shakes her head, to my mind unsupportively. She says, "Honey, you have one mighty imagination; you ought to write a play, a book or at least a short story."

She never was a fan of the triathlon trainers, but she thinks I exaggerate their unkindness. She doubts they are upset with me, she guesses their problems stem from something personal at home, perhaps financial or sexual. "Something about people paying so much attention to themselves seems, well, frigid. In any case, it is surely not sexy," she says one evening. The older twins are with the younger ones at the park, I am doing sit-ups and lunges, listening to her rehearse. She adds, "And you don't even read the newspapers anymore, Bry. In fact, I never see you read anything anymore."

Bitty, irritatingly, has a habit of almost always being right and she knows it. I said it before but I will say it again: *Harvest* gives me something not just to think about and engage with, but something to love. I cannot bring myself to love triathlon training. I love *Harvest;* love its sentences, its landscapes and people. But at a certain point I cannot rekindle that vital connection. I know the scenes, the dialogue, the story, and the stories within them. I know them and love them, but it is an old, familiar love that will not take me anywhere new. It pulls me back. It becomes something nostalgic, something to dwell on. And I understand how tricky nostalgia can be, how, in a heartbeat, it turns into an enemy; turns into something that lets you mope, hide out in the past, avoid the uncertainty of what is now. I've got to figure out something new to make.

So, I decide to try to come up with a story, or at least rework another story.

Years and years ago, in college, I visit northern Michigan with my roommate, Ellen. That trip really sticks with me, unpleasantly, for different reasons, only some of which I understand.

From the minute I meet Ellen she goes on and on about her home state Michigan; how pretty it is, how diverse, how romantic. How different seasons offer every single kind of weather (snowy winters, sunny summers, languid, fragrant spring days, crisp fall ones). This constant Michigan talk irritates some of the students on my floor but I understand it this way: Ellen is homesick, and expresses that longing by talking endlessly about her home.

She convinces me to travel to Michigan with her over spring break.

Maybe she sets the bar too high, maybe I am, at that time, unused to travel, maybe I miss Euge, but the trip is not, for me, enjoyable. In fact, I find the whole visit creepy.

What is the root of my Michigan problem? It might have something to do with landscape. She is from the rural, northern part of the state. I, at that point, am used to rural areas that, like my town, are flat; you can see everything for miles and miles. The land surrounding her northern Michigan home has so many and such different terrains: hills, lakes, valleys, rivers, ponds, fields, puddles, and so many kinds of foliage. I remember her house being near a lake and on a piece of property dense with trees, bushes and streams. It is so crowded you cannot really see anything. I mean, you can see the separate things on the property but you never know what else is there, behind all those leaves and trees and stumps. You can never see the whole picture. No one can hide in my flat town, or its surrounding area. But anyone or anything can hide in those Michigan woods.

Her parents are nice, from what I remember, but they are only home one night before heading off to a camping trip. They wear tie-dyed shirts; have long hair and a garden of vegetables and marijuana plants. They invite us to go on their trip with them but Ellen rolls her eyes, explaining she and I want to be in the house alone, and she wants me to meet her friends. That first night, before dinner, her dad (full beard, thick-soled sandals) takes us in the backyard, asks if we want to join him and smoke some pot. We both decline. He smokes, talks. At some point he kneels down, shows us an ant hole, tells us ant holes are perilous, fragile things to honor and respect. He says wise men call ant holes the earth's ear. After he says this he bows his head for several minutes of silence. Ellen looks at me, shakes her head, mouths, "Sorry…"

Ellen and I spend the rest of our week there hiking, and visiting her friends. One tells me his father has a weapon stockpile. We spend most evenings at her town's bowling alley listening and dancing to loud rock and roll music.

I still feel so badly about my reaction to Michigan, and to her. The more time I spend thinking about things I regret, the longer the list seems to grow.

"Regret is one of the hazardous temptations of aging," my father-in-law tells me. "Don't indulge, it makes you old, quick."

There I go again, indulging. If it is not in one thing it is in another. If it is not worrying about my ability as a mother, or as a stepmother, or my tendency to become harshly judgmental when I do not have anything interesting to do or think about, it is recounting mistakes I made in college.

Another thing I do on that visit to Ellen's home in northern Michigan is read. I read, and then re-read a ghost story, *The Turn of the Screw,* by Henry James. Maybe that jinxes my visit. That eerie little masterpiece. I come back to it now, years later, in fact it is the first thing I read after I quit, I mean stop, triathlon training. I then read it again and again. I become absorbed in it and decide to interact with it, or to try to. I absolutely cannot write like Henry James just like I cannot write like Ernest. James' book is about being lonely, and scared, in the wilderness. Two sensations I have visiting Ellen in Michigan. And then there is the whole question of the governess: does she truly encounter things supernatural; does she make things up?

And I feel the need to spend more time with things creepy. Fear can serve as a distraction.

I read somewhere – I think in college – that if a child is in the midst of a tantrum, a firm but gentle shake can pull him or her out of it. A jolt. This is what creepiness does for me. Jolts. Maybe if I let myself be fearful, instead of restricting my mental activity, I can work something out of my system. The older twins love horror films, are always telling me that horror is a major release for them, and probably could be for me, if I would ever just let myself experience it. I am too frightened to really watch or read something frightening. I cover my eyes, close my book and leave the room. Admittedly, I have a problem really handling horror. For one thing, I start thinking about the Demon. I always wind up feeling sorry for the evil person or character, believing he or she was terribly abused as a child, events that help explain behavior, even if the explanation does not excuse it. I always want to find something good in these people, something good that was squashed with vicious beatings or endless periods of neglect, something to account for developed, behavioral monstrosity. Bitty tells me if I was ever the victim of a brutal crime, or if my children were, I would change my tune. She is likely right. My opinion probably only reflects my lack of experience, and my unwillingness to look at stark reality.

I have always been afraid of exploring the dark side of things, but here is why: I am afraid that if I think of something bad it will happen, my thinking just might turn the thought into fact. I am not saying this is a good way of thinking, just that it is how I think.

Demons and criminals are unwelcome and frightening to think about, but in fact it is things like car accidents, heart disease and cancer that wind up endangering or killing most of us.

I know I am rambling here, recording this information in my sturdy, leather-bound journal. This is probably because I sense it is time for me to start a new project, to switch over to a flimsy, inexpensive, lined notebook. I understand that I take time, too much time, relating unimportant things, probably because I do not know how to communicate things truly important. Truly important would be, for example, making up something creative and engaging. I am not saying I am, or ever will be, able to invent something structurally sound, ringing with horror, pathos or beauty. But I enjoy making up good company.

2.5
THE TURN OF THE NORTH

*Someone would appear there at the turn of a path
and would stand before me and smile and approve.*
HENRY JAMES

When you have everything, you have everything to lose.
BEN HARPER

2002

WEDNESDAY

We finally reach our place up north, stiff and cold after the long drive. It is a chilly, early fall evening. The leaves, some turned, are still on trees. By we I mean: my cousin Sue and I, and our children. It is Wednesday. Saturday our husbands (mine, Joe; hers, my cousin Frankie) will drive up together. Because the kids will miss two days of school, we bring their backpacks, stuffed with textbooks and folders of homework.

We visit our cabin every year at this time to prepare it for winter, and to re-wire the property before the start of hunting season. Hunting is a part of life in this northern area of our state, but we do not condone it on our land. Good hunters will not trespass. At regular intervals, about 90 feet, we tack bright-colored triangles onto trees above the wire for visibility. Most landowners up here re-wire once a year. When my cousins and

I were children, our fathers did this. As we grew older, they brought us with them. Now, with my father dead, one uncle living permanently down south, and another very sick, the job—at least until our kids are older—is ours. Or, more accurately, Joe and Frankie's. The piece of property, eighty acres, in Northern Michigan, on Lake Huron, near a small town named Kappon, has been in our family for generations. We do not lock our doors, we keep our keys in the car, and we are friendly with neighbors. Our closest neighbor, Marie, lives on the lake a quarter of a mile down the road. Our children call her Granny.

We only once had security trouble at our cabin. About four years ago we found it ransacked. Nothing was stolen or broken, but plates had been used, beds slept in. Empty beer and liquor bottles and cigarette butts littered our floor and tables. We called the police who came out, inspected the damage, and filed a report. It took them a good half hour to get here. They told us that a group of motorcyclists ride through the county from time to time and vandalize. My cousin Frankie then decided we should keep a gun around, reasoning that if any of us are here, in the cabin, and vandals attack, we clearly cannot count on police protection.

We keep the gun inside the standing cedar cupboard that holds stacked dishes, neatly folded holiday linens, and boxes of seasonal decorations. When Frankie is here he puts it in the drawer next to his bed. Joe, Sue, and I understand why he believes we need a weapon, but we all worry. We worry mostly for the safety of our children. They are obedient kids, however. We show them where we keep the gun and give strict orders never to touch it.

Frankie is, and has always been, my favorite cousin.

On this fall evening we get to our cabin, unpack and grill hamburgers. After dinner the kids play a board game, Sue and I drink bottles of beer and say how glad we are to be sleeping here, in this fresh air, how it bothers us that neighbors downstate rely so heavily on leaf blowers (horrendous, loud), and on pesticides, which make the air so bad, and give our kids asthma and who knows what other kinds of ailments.

THURSDAY

My dream just before waking: I am wrapped tightly around my husband Joe; he holds my head in his hands. I am saddened to wake up and find myself alone in this big bed, overlooking our lawn, our beach and the lake, but brighten up when I remember Joe will be here soon. We sleep in one of the two main bedrooms upstairs, at the front of the cabin, and Frank and Sue sleep in the other one. On the backside of the hallway are three smaller bedrooms. Above this floor is the loft area where the kids now sleep. Walking out of my room, the room I usually share with Joe, I notice that Sue's door is open. I leave mine open too. I climb up the ladder to the loft, check all of the children in their beds. At some point in the night these cousins always pile into one bed. Now I view their heads and feet and arms, together with the pillows and blankets, as one tangle. Someone snores but I cannot tell whom. Sue is up. For the next hour, we do calisthenics on the lawn between the cabin and the lake. When we have finished, the children are still sleeping. We go inside, cook our ritual up-north breakfast:

eggs, juice, coffee, side pork and muffins. Sue cooks the eggs and side pork. She shows me a new way she cracks eggs. Rather than tapping them on the side of her fry pan, she now taps them on the countertop before breaking them into pan. This, she says, lessens the chance of broken shells getting into the eggs. I bake the muffins using a batch of quick-bread dry mix Sue put together last month and kept in our freezer. The kids come downstairs, take their plates of food outside. After their meal, Sue walks them down the beach to Marie's, and drives into town for groceries. I line two baskets with paper towels, take them in the woods; one is for herbs, one for wild mushrooms. Tonight we are making beef stew.

It is easy for me to get lost in the woods when the season is fall. When I say lost I do not mean geographically. I mean getting lost in the crisp air and colors, along with the odd symmetries of our forest's landscape.

After about an hour, I find what I will need for tonight's stew, and am ready to head home. I realize I have not seen a single mosquito. This time of the year they are not out in droves, but it is unusual not to encounter one. Wanting to spend more time in the woods, especially since it seems so bug-free, I walk over to the river that runs through our property. My husband and children come up here for the great lake. I love that lake, yet I never feel settled-in until I visit the river. Walking down the sloped path toward it, through cedar, pine and oak trees, I am alarmed to see, standing on the river bank, a green tent. Two portable canvas travel chairs, on either side of a table made of the same material, stand in front of it. A thermos with a red plaid design is on the table. It is not a freestanding tent, back-packed in by a hiker. It is a larger, more permanent structure, held up by two big poles, anchored by stakes dug into our ground.

My heart starts to pound and I feel my cheeks turning red. I stand up straight, pull in my stomach and walk back to our cabin as quickly as I can.

Walking home I find myself excited by what I saw. Excited and also hopeful. But I cannot let my expectations rise too high.

When I reach our cabin, no one is there. I expect this. Sue is probably back from town, but over at Marie's, with the kids. I lean against our sink, put the herbs in a bowl of water, wipe off mushrooms, try to remember if I saw any today that could have been poison. A poisonous mushroom, as I have told Frankie, can be a far more dangerous weapon than a gun.

I open the refrigerator and see that Sue has stocked it with supplies: jugs of juice, packets of turkey and bacon, two gallons of milk, a carton of eggs. Sue keeps eggs in their store-container, rather than putting them in the tray on the side of our refrigerator door, because she believes that the temperature by the door is too low. Also in our refrigerator is a ceramic baking dish of beef Sue has cubed and salted.

It is late afternoon when she returns with the children. Calmed after raking a pile of leaves and sweeping off our front and back porch, I greet her. We get busy. Our children are starving and cannot wait to tell me about their day with Marie and their hike along the beach. We make dinner: mushroom and beef stew, potatoes, cornbread, and a beet and cucumber salad. When we are here we take our time, which means most things, meals included, are long and pleasant. At home, downstate, it seems as if we barely have time to sit down and finish eating before heading out to some other scheduled activity. But up here we do not have those distractions. The kids take turns telling stories and jokes, and doing imitations of their teachers from school. Our dining table faces a window that overlooks the lake. As the evening goes on we realize that tonight there is a nearly full moon, and a dense, starry sky. When dinner is over the children help us clean up, then beg us to come outside with them. The four cousins climb onto our large hammock. For a long time Sue and I stand there with them staring at the sky, gently swinging the hammock. I almost forget about the tent. At some point we realize two of the children have fallen asleep and it is definitely time for bed. We walk them up to the loft and tuck them in.

Downstairs in the kitchen, over small glasses of whiskey, we discuss the day, our husbands. I do not tell Sue about the tent, I cannot. I think I know who erected it but I also understand that might be my own wishful thinking and also that they are not the sort of wishes I should necessarily be having.

1970

I hate being up north. It is boring and cold in the winter, hot and buggy in the summer. The water—we pump from a well, the pump is red—tastes like dirt and stones.

I hate being here. I wish I were in a town, or near one. I wish I could find a place to buy soda pop and candy, wish I could go see a movie, wish I were at home, playing with my friends.

Instead I am up north in the woods, dirty, sweating, getting
bitten by mosquitoes. I hate the woods. I am angry with my
family: boy cousins and my parents. My parents force me to
come up here even though they know I hate it. I have all boy
cousins, no girls, and they spend their time playing sports or
wrestling with each other. They do not ever want to play with
me. I do not want to play with them either. They are too rough,
too smelly, too loud and mean. I carry a box holding my dolls
and different doll outfits on my walk in the woods. I love my
grandparents but they are not always here. And when they
are here, they stay in the cabin on the lake. That is better than
where we stay, in the woods. Their Lake Cabin has breezes and
you can always swim. They have running water and an indoor
toilet. If I had to come up north and had the chance to stay
at their Lake Cabin instead of the Woods Cabin I don't think
I would mind it so much. The cabin in the woods, where my
parents force me to stay, has an outhouse and we have to pump
water. There are no screens on the windows. It is scary at night.
My grandparents say I can stay with them whenever I want
but my parents do not want me to. They like staying in a small
cabin in dark woods, and want me to have this experience too.
"Honey," they say when I complain, they say this holding hands
and smiling at one another, "most kids never get a real camping
experience. Look at all you have learned, doing things with
nature. You have chopped down trees, stripped and notched
them. You helped build a whole cabin. Who else in your class
at school can say that? You helped dig the well, make a fire, get
water from the stream and boil it to wash dishes. Find herbs and

mushrooms. Fish in the stream. You are learning survival. This is what people had to do before modern conveniences came around. Even if you don't enjoy it you are learning history."

This is a lecture I get, or a version of it, whenever I complain about being here, or ask if I can please sleep at Grandma and Grandpa's. More than anything my parents hate complaints. Won't listen to them. Change the subject. And let me make something clear: I never chopped down a tree. I might have taken one swing with my dad or uncle's axe. And I did not dig a well. I might have taken one scoop of mud out with a shovel. I hate my parents. I hate the drive to this cabin. We leave a nice paved road and turn down a twisty, bumpy one-lined road with dense trees. I turn around and look out the back window of our van at that paved road. "Shut the window, don't let in the mosquitoes," my parents say. Easy for them to joke about this. They do not seem to ever get bitten by mosquitoes. I always get bitten. My legs, neck, arms, face. They don't care. They only see what happens to them. They never see what happens to me. "I wish you got bit by mosquitoes," I told my dad. "Then you'd emphasize."

"Emphasize? Emphasize…"

"No, I meant empathize, PA-thize."

Too late.

"Hey honey," he says to mom, "did you hear that? She said emphasize." Then, turning to me, "No one needs to do that around here, it seems as if you are emphasizing, very strongly, that you do not like it here."

I turn red.

"You KNOW that is not what I meant, I meant em-pa-thize. But you never listen when I talk to you. I hate you DAD. DAD, STOP TEASING ME!"

"Calm down, hey, I am not, I am not I mean it...I like when you use big words, or try to use them, wait, no, I mean...."

I storm out the van when we stop. I hope he feels bad, terrible, even.

"She is so over-sensitive, especially when we are here," I hear my mom tell him and I run into the woods.

This is what happened on the first day I saw the tent and met the two boys who stayed there.

I walk in the woods by myself. No one will miss me. I always feel stupid around my father. He loves to tease when people say things that are stupid. I meant to say empathize and said emphasize. I can be sure this story will be told, again and again, to all of my parents' friends and relatives, and when they tell the story they will say something about how much I read and use vocabulary. Right now I bet my cousins are wrestling with each other, my mom, dad, aunt and uncle are diagramming plans for another cabin, probably farther in the woods, they all want to build here, and talking about how sensitive and what a good reader I am. My family can never just say one thing about someone, they have to always say at least two different things.

I cannot just be a good reader, I have to be overly sensitive too. I am not only overly sensitive—I have a strength: good reader (!) too. It drives me crazy. It drives me crazy in the same way when we come up here we can never just stay in our grandparents' big, cool, cabin that gets a good wind and very few bugs because it is on a great lake. We have to stay in these hot woods where these adults can't wait to chop down trees, strip and notch the logs so they can build more and more small structures.

Even if my cousins say I am invited to play with them I know that they play hard and rough and throw footballs between each other and sticks for the dog and I feel as if I would cut into their fun because I am not good at any of those things.

I walk in the woods by myself. I unwrap the jawbreaker I brought from home and hid in my sweatshirt pocket. My parents and aunts and uncles are obsessed with their idea of health food. We had oatmeal for breakfast (a clumpy bowl of raisins was also on the table), lentil soup and carrots for lunch. We do not eat this way at home. There we eat normal food: toast, chicken, potatoes, corn and ice cream. If my grandparents are up here we eat this way too. Something happens when my parents and aunts and uncles are here on their own. Now, having pretty much skipped breakfast and lunch, I suck on my jawbreaker (it is a fireball, just now getting really, really hot) and feel dizzy as I walk through the woods, imagining all of the different kinds of families I could have besides the one I am stuck with.

I walk to the river. Today it is pretty shallow. I walk toward it and I see a boy sitting on a tree stump. I know this particular stump because my dad and uncle were very proud when they chopped down the tree it was a part of last year. In fact, it was the scene of a large family photo. Within a minute I see two boys. One sits on the stump, the other stands behind it. They look alike but wear different colored shirts.

"Hi," one in an orange t-shirt says. "I am Chris, this is Dave." Dave wears a green shirt. "Ah, hi," I say, moving my jawbreaker to the back of one cheek. They look a little older than my older cousins. They both stand up. I can see Chris is shorter than Dave. "What is in your mouth?" asks the one named Chris. "Fireball," I answer. "Yes, your mouth and lips look blood red," says the one named Dave.

I swat a mosquito that has just bit my knee. "Come inside the tent," says Dave. I see he is really tall, so tall he has to stoop to get inside the tent. He goes on to say it is cool there and there are no bugs. We go in. The floor is covered with wooden blocks. Some are stacked into shapes of forts and buildings. In a corner there is a cooler filled with cans of soda pop. They offer me one. Ginger ale. "Thanks," I tell them. The bubbles tickle my nose. There are piles of books. I look at them. All boy adventure stories, like the ones my cousins read. I love to read but not those books. Those books are boring. There is nothing about talking or listening or thinking, just moving quickly from one thing to another. I open my doll box. "Those girls need a home," says Chris. We all start to work, making buildings with the blocks. "Let's make an A-Frame," says Chris. "And they can have a swimming pool," says Dave. "And a boat house." They finish the Boat House first. My dolls like being in there. I like being in the tent. We play for the whole afternoon. I start to get hungry. I hear a gong. "This is the time your family eats dinner. I will walk you toward there," says Dave. Chris stays in the tent, working on my dolls' A-frame. On our way to the cabin I can see, through the thick trees, that the sky is turning gold. I mention this to Dave who says gold is his and Chris's favorite color.

"Who brings you here?" I ask.

"Our Uncle," Dave answers.

When we reach our cabin, "Goodbye."

I stand, staring at him, wanting to give him a hug.

He leans toward me.

"You know," he whispers, "you have everything we want. Just keep that in mind. Don't let it make you feel bad, just try to understand that."

I hear him run through the woods.

I want to run after him because I am very angry, almost as angry as I was with my father earlier today, only I expected to get angry with my father, I never expected to get angry with my new friend Dave. I HAVE NOTHING I WANT, I want to scream back at him. NOTHING. YOU ON THE OTHER HAND HAVE A NICE BROTHER YOU CAN PLAY WITH AND GOOD THINGS TO DRINK AND A TENT, PROTECTION FROM BUGS AND RAIN. YOU HAVE A GOOD UNCLE WHO BRINGS YOU PLACES AND MAKES SURE YOU CAN ACTUALLY HAVE FUN IN THEM. I hear boys talking. It is my cousins, covered in dirt, walking to the cabin. "Hey," says my cousin Frankie. "Come with us and eat." I follow them.

At "home" everyone sits on logs eating dinner (water from a well, noodles, mushrooms, rice cakes). Not one adult had even noticed I was gone. Of course. And my parents do not remember what sent me away in the first place or at least do not bring up anything about *emphasize* or *empathize*. They have other interests. They hand me a glass and plate and talk, as darkness closes in all around us, about how they will have to wire off the property this fall, and how much I will learn from helping them, how they hate we have to leave tomorrow. My cousins eat quickly and play a game with a fluorescent ball. I do not say anything about the brothers. The boys, their tent, the blocks, give me something to think about. When I have something to think about, I can forget the bad food, dirt and bugs. Also, I finally have something up here in the woods I can keep all to myself.

"You have everything we want." I think about this as I fall asleep.

What could that mean? We really don't have very much. As a family, we aren't good company. We eat bad food, are not very well-dressed or good-looking. We drive an old car with no air-conditioning.

The next morning I wake up. On the pillow is a boat, whittled from a piece of wood. On the bottom someone carved: DOLL BOAT HOUSE PROPERTY.

I believe the brothers left it. I need to thank them.

I know we are leaving, but I want to say goodbye and thank Chris and Dave. I run to their tent. They are sitting outside on a stump whittling sticks. "Hi," I say, turning red. I can't remember what I wanted to tell them. "Uhm," I say, "thank you." I show them the boat and how my doll fits right in it. Chris leans over to me and says I can stop getting bitten by mosquitoes if I rub the boat up and down my legs, especially on the insides, but without the doll in it.

On our drive home I think about them but do not say anything. I do not even tell Frankie. I know what he would say. That I always make things up, and that the boys probably just live in the nearby town.

2002

FRIDAY

I wake up around 5:30 in the dark, thinking about Joe. I remember a long time ago, comparing him to the brothers, Chris and Dave, and even to my cousin Frankie. Downstate Joe is the perfect man. But when I am up here, sometimes, I feel as though he falls short. Joe is usual. Frankie is less usual. Chris and Dave are unusual. Sometimes Joe's usualness irritates me and I stop wanting to talk to him or to listen to anything he has to say. But this morning I miss him and am glad he is coming soon.

I am nervous and sometimes detailing things calms me down. Let me describe the room Joe and I usually sleep in. Our cabin is a log cabin. So picture a room with a pitched ceiling and horizontal log walls. Our bed is a four-poster, wood frame. On it is a red-and-black-checkered blanket. We use this blanket for warmth in cool weather, but in the summer it just stays folded at the foot of the bed for decoration. There are several small, oval weave rugs on the floor. A broom stands next to the door. Cabins get very dusty and when we come up here, we sweep and dust a lot. We have a closet.

Our cabin faces the lake. We have a big yard in front of and behind our cabin. Behind the back yard is a paved road that heads into town. Behind that road lies the rest of our property. I always feel safe running along this road, even in the dark. It is never busy, but it is never dead; there is always a car or two passing down it, whatever the time of day or night. This morning I run two miles in one direction, then turn and run the same distance back. By this time it is getting light. I walk over to our beach, skip rope and look out at the glassy morning water. It is too cool to swim. Rays of sunlight shine through our tall trees. I put down my jump rope and use the bench of our picnic table to do some push-ups and triceps dips. I finish with a series of stretches. I feel awake, refreshed, walk inside the cabin. Sue stands at the counter, making biscuits. We eat them with local organic honey. We started doing this when Marie suggested eating local organic honey is a way to improve allergies. My daughter is allergic to bees and both Sue's children cannot eat the skin of peaches. Something in the fuzz of that skin gives them hives. They also get sick from onions. The onions do not give them hives, just sore throats. So we give them a spoon of organic honey every day unless we use it in some other kind of food like cereal or these biscuits.

 The four children are upstairs, in bed, talking, whispering and singing. Sue pours me a large mug of coffee. We sit together on the front porch, talking about our husbands. How we are, and are not, glad they are coming up tomorrow. All at once, the kids are downstairs. Sue has already set out cereal, milk and juice. Now she takes her biscuits out of the oven. "Have some biscuits with your honey," we hear my son, who does not have a sweet tooth, say to his sister and cousins. Sue and I go out to the porch, and start planning next summer's garden. We also agree that the daily local organic honey does not seem to be relieving anyone's allergies. After breakfast the kids go outside to the tree house, make us promise we will roast marshmallows this evening. Sue and I wash the dishes, sweep, dust, and make the beds.

We have a lot to do to prepare, since we plan to be here later this fall, as well as for Thanksgiving and Christmas. Sue has made a list: unpack flannel sheets and warm blankets. Wash the sheets and hang the blankets out to air. Bring the boxes of hats and socks and gloves in from the garage and place them in a bin by the front door. Also bring in the boots. Take down and wash the curtains. Purchase what we need to stock our pantry and our cellar and freezer. Make sure we have salt to put on the driveway. Check snow shovels.

One winter both of our shovels had broken handles. There was a heavy snow. Joe and Frankie had to use the shovels with just little bits of sticks for handles, which meant they had to crouch down. It was hard on their knees and backs (though they would never say so). Since then we always check to make sure there are no cracks on the wood handles.

When there is a heavy snow someone usually says, "We should get a snow-blower." But we never do. If the snow becomes too deep are very deep we can always hire someone from the community to clear it.

Joe and Frank will not only rewire our land when they get here, but also chop and stack wood. We try to use our woodstove for heat and for cooking as much as we can.

Frank's dad and mine were brothers. His dad is living down south. At least once a season, he comes up to visit. He has become a passionate golfer. In fact, he and our moms (mine and Frankie's) are on a golf trip this fall, in Scotland. They will all join us here on Thanksgiving.

I hated coming up here when I was younger, at the time. But now, looking back, I am glad I did. I have some nice memories. Swimming for hours in the lake, the way our children do now. We especially loved when the waters were choppy and we could ride the waves. Long meals, sitting in front of a campfire, telling stories, roasting marshmallows. And my parents taught me a lot about surviving in the woods. Our kids love it here. But of course, they never have to sleep in the Woods Cabin, like I did. At the time I was not wild about it but now, looking back, I think of it differently. If I had not had to stay there, I would never have met Chris and Dave. They changed my life, even though I spent very little time with them, by giving me so much to think about.

Just before lunch we all walk down the beach to call upon Marie. We walk her back to our place, serve up lunch: soup, apples, and Sue's biscuits. Marie brings a jug of cider. She asks if the organic honey is improving our children's allergies and we both answer, "Yes."

She gives a knowing nod and tucks into her soup. I know Sue and I, later, will talk about how we both always want to please Marie, even if it means telling her something untrue. Although the honey may be helping the allergies, we do not have evidence, yet to be fair we cannot say for certain. We eat at our table on our screened-in porch. It is a cool, windless, overcast day. The water is gray and still. After lunch Marie asks to take our kids back with her for a visit. We say ok but as long as the kids take their homework. Marie is a retired schoolteacher and understands how to help children finish homework thoroughly and quickly. Homework is something Sue and I talk about continually: the massive amounts of math, science, and language arts pages assigned to our children. It eats into our family time in the evenings, on weekends and vacations. And some of their assignments are so complex we don't have a clue how to help them. But Marie does and she is happy to. We watch them walk down the beach, lugging their backpacks. Once again I think of how unhealthy it is for my small, thin children to carry such massive weight on their little shoulders, of the strain it puts on their developing skeletal structures.

Just as we clear the lunch plates off the table on our screened-in porch, we get a visit from Don, our friend and caretaker. He is Marie's brother and lives down the beach from her. We give him a plate of Sue's biscuits, a cup of coffee. He is a teacher, married with two children. He asks if we notice the mosquito level has dropped. I say yes, I had that thought during my walk in the woods yesterday. He explains it is probably because of the bat houses he and Marie have put up all around their property and ours. I do not pay attention to this at the time, only think about it later, but tell him I am going to look for mushrooms and herbs in the woods and ask if he wants to come with me. He agrees. What I really want to do, in addition to getting his help looking for mushrooms (Don has an eagle eye), is to see if the tent is still there. We take our time walking through the woods.

There is nothing more beautiful, Don and I agree, than our woods in the fall. The colors, the smells, the sounds of birds. I walk him to the exact spot by the river where I saw the tent yesterday. No tent. No indentations where I saw four sturdy stakes were, just yesterday, plunged deep into our ground. I am shocked, disappointed and want to cry. I crouch down and pull up some herbs, hoping Don cannot see my tears. He is looking up at the trees. He touches my shoulder. "See, that is one of our bat houses. We put them on your property as well. That is why we don't have mosquitoes. The bats get them. People forget bats are protection."

After about a half of a mile, we come across a different tent. Nowhere near where I saw the previous one. It is not the same tent I saw yesterday. This one is smaller. A pup tent, not a large, expansive tent.

"Now what do you think about this?" asks Don.

"Uhm," I answer. We stand there. He squats down, examines the stakes.

"This tent has been pitched here for awhile. You see how the dirt has covered this metal? It is a new tent but these stakes are far from shiny. They are used to the dirt. Look here," he continues, "a campfire." Behind the tent are a small circle of rocks and a neatly piled stack of wood in the center. Next to it, on a stump, is a blue coffee pot and an iron skillet.

"Yep," says Don, "someone is making this a home, at least for awhile."

"Uhm," I say, "Are you going to look inside?"

"No," he shakes his head. "No."

"Do you think it is one person or that it could be two people?" I ask.

"Hard to say," he answers.

We walk deeper in the woods. He talks about how fall is his favorite season, but it is dangerous because the hunters come out. He wears bright orange today, even though it is before hunting season. He believes one can never be too careful in these woods. He says he is glad Frank and Joe are coming to rewire the land. He talks about how this part of the state has been hit hard by a bad economy. How there are no jobs. How the kids in his school have a hard time getting dental care. He says that hunting, gardening and fishing help people get by because they do not have to depend on grocery stores. On the other hand, a big grocery store in Kappon just closed. Now residents have to drive fifteen minutes farther unless they want to go to the liquor store or gas station. I have heard Don say this before and do not mind hearing him say it again. Don is a teacher and used to talking for long periods. It is hard to converse with Don because he tends to lecture. It is because of his teaching. I like listening to him, though. He has a soothing voice and is one of the kindest people I've ever known.

"Look here! Chanterelles."

"We were going for those but you can go ahead and have them," a voice from behind us says. We turn around. There they stand. Two men. I know them. Chris and Dave, grown up. My throat fills up. They stand just a few feet away. I can see their boots and the bottoms of their jeans are wet.

"Oh, no, you are welcome to them..." I stumble, feeling prickly and overly warm. My voice feels high pitched and out of control. Frantic.

"Good fishing?" Don asks, nodding to the bucket on the ground between them. We see some tails sticking up over the top.

I know these two people. I cannot remember when I last saw them. I can barely believe I am seeing them now. I not only know them, I love them. I LOVE THEM. ALL THIS TIME AND IT IS STILL TRUE. I am not sure what to do. They are handsome grown ups. Both wear baseball caps (Detroit Tigers) pushed back so I have a clear view of their faces. Red hair curls down around round cheeks, dark, and arched eyebrows, large blue eyes. They stand tall and erect. I get the idea that they are actors or professional athletes.

"Hi," I say, trying to lower my voice.

"Hi," they answer, both at once.

"Chris, Dave?" I ask?

"Nope," the tall one says, smiling. They shake their heads, stare at me deep and hard.

"Oh," I say. "You look like two boys I used to know."

"Well we should," the smaller one answers. "We are actors. Actors are supposed to always look like other people, and behave like them too."

"You think you know them from when?" asks Don

"Uhm...do you want these?" I ask the actors, pointing to the mushrooms.

"Yes," says Don, as if I am talking to him, "I very much want these." He kneels down and pulls the mushrooms gently from the earth, places them in his basket, lips pinched together.

"Well," says the shorter one I know is Chris, "You get to take what you want." Don is involved in the mushrooms. He does not look at me but, finally, stands up. The four of us walk a ways together.

"Bye now" the tall one (Dave) says when we reach the road. "We go this way," and they walk to the right. He swings his bucket of fish. Don and I walk toward the road.

"Do you think it was their tent we saw?" I ask.

"Hard to say," he answers.

We find more mushrooms.

I fight between different kinds of feelings: sad and excited. Those two are Chris and Dave but they do not acknowledge that fact or even that they know me. This could be a compliment, a form of protection, a promise to keep our secret.

But it could also mean that they have lost interest in me and the things we used to do.

FRIDAY (STILL)

Don and I walk back to the cabin. I am sad, and feel my posture slumping, which probably broadcasts my feelings of sadness. Don does not, would not, notice, but the brothers may be lurking around somewhere and anyway we might run into someone we know. I try to hold my stomach in and stand up straight but find it hard going. When I first met Chris and Dave, I was young and did not have any responsibilities. I was also bored. It had been a long time since I thought about how bored I was as a child, especially when spending time up here. Everyone else seemed so busy. I could never find anything I liked to do. I sort of hung around and everyone ignored me. Being ignored made me sad but it was also a time I could be left alone with my thoughts. That was one of the best things about Chris and Dave. They gave me things to think about. Now I would love to be ignored. But no. Now, everyone always wants something and all I want to do sometimes, this minute for example, is be alone and think. I want to think about Chris and Dave and try to decipher what they are doing. Now, no one ever leaves me alone, including Sue. Let me explain what I mean by no one leaves me alone including Sue. I love Sue. In fact, I wish I were more like her. Sue is a healthy person, and like many healthy people she thrives on interpersonal contact. If she has a choice between being by herself or being with people, any people, she will choose the latter. She loves company. I am not like that. I have, well, problems. I need time to sort those problems, and things in general, out. I need time by myself. I enjoy being around people, but the contact really drains me. I need to get away and refuel. Still, I love Sue and she never irritates me the way some others tend to. It is just that I feel guilty when I want to be alone. I don't know how to tell her in a way that will not hurt her feelings. And boy do I have a lot to think about right now with The Brothers. What do they do? Are they really actors? Where do they live? Do they have lovers, wives and children?

Evening comes around. I leave Sue and Don in the kitchen, watching the evening news. I walk out to the sandy beach, sit down in the large deck chair facing the lake, wait. I have a feeling that I know what is going to happen. It is that time of the day, the sky turns a sort of gold, and I expect to see the brothers run out of the woods and into the water. Sure enough, within moments, they come running out of the woods, arms linked running into the freezing cold Lake Huron. They stop at the water's edge and scream, "YES" as icy waves lap over their shins and thighs and torsos. They dive into the water, swim out far. I see them do jumping jacks, handstands, flips in the water. After awhile they return to the beach, do some more calisthenics. I believe that they do the same routine Sue and I did the other morning. They take one last plunge in the lake. I cannot stop watching them. I notice they have muscular arms, wear tight, short sleeve shirts, have erect nipples. They walk toward me on the reclining beach chair. I stand up, wonder if Sue and Dan are going to see any of this from the house, and ask the brothers if they want to come inside and join us for a beer.

"We don't drink," they both answer at once.

"Well," I answer, "I mean, you can have other things besides beer to drink: water or something warm…"

"You misunderstand. We do not drink. Anything. Liquid turns solid in our mouths," says Chris.

"How do you hydrate?"

"We absorb liquids through our skin. This is one reason why swimming is so important," says Chris.

"And the rain, the snow," says Dave.

After awhile I ask, "Well, do you want to come in for a visit?"

"Another time. We have some fruit to rinse, some mushrooms to fry," says Chris.

They turn around, jog back into the woods.

I stand on the beach, look out at the horizon. The lake is gray and choppy.

SATURDAY

I get up and run small circles around our cabin until my odometer reads 3 miles. I feel hopeful, but not happy. Hopeful that Chris and Dave are in the woods, watching me. If they are I will feel happy. If they are not I will feel bad. Very bad. Not knowing makes me anxious, and I do not have the skills to cope with this kind of anxiety. Hope can be a good thing, but if indulged, it can debilitate. Or that is my personal experience.

What happens to me is this: I get excited about the possibility of something (in this case, the brothers watching me), then become deeply saddened when it does not take place. I believe that the difference between me—a mildly successful person—and a truly successful person is this: a truly successful person is able to maintain a sense of heightened expectation and not experience crushing disappointment when that hope is not met.

It is unlikely the brothers are even up and about yet. Not everyone wakes up early, ready to charge into the world, like I do. This is something Joe and Sue have helped me to understand. Joe rarely wakes up with energy. Sue may get up and exercise with me one day, but then the next she will sleep in. Not me. I wake up every day, needing to move.

What do the brothers mean that they do not drink anything? You cannot be human and not drink anything. Skin absorption is an incomplete hydration method. Esophageal tissue is nourished when liquids pass through it, and that happens only, as far as I know, when swallowing. The brothers, telling me they only absorb liquids is their way of joking or of tilting things off balance. Now I remember this about them. You can never tell if they are joking or just being bizarre to knock you off kilter. It happened often that one would say something I thought was funny and I would laugh, but neither of them laughed or smiled back.

For example, that afternoon when the two of them took me on a speedboat up the coast to get ice cream. It was a hot summer and my parents were not using ice so we drank well water or warm juice. That summer they cooked skillet-fried salt pork and potatoes over the campfire every night, sometimes with eggs. I told the brothers I was sick of eating such heavy warm food; I was thirsty and wanted something cold. We walked out of the woods to the beach. They pointed to a red speedboat anchored out a ways in the water.

I had never seen something so beautiful, especially here, and said so.

"It is ours. Our uncle gave it to us. Let's walk out and get in," said Chris. Assuming he was kidding I laughed, "Right-OH." He and his brother stared at me, silent. "If you don't want to ride with us you don't have to," said Dave unhappily.

This sense of not knowing, of dislocation, is characteristic of how they used to make me feel: dizzy. Like things were spinning and I was going to fall over. In their presence, things familiar (words, hand gestures, eye contact) were used in ways that were new to me. That time, though, I waded out with them to the boat, got in, and rode around with them all afternoon. They took me to a place up the coast. We ordered ginger ale ice cream floats. It was the best eating experience of that whole summer. Another time, in the winter, they took me somewhere on a snowmobile. I complained about how we had to stay in the cabin, and how all we ate one weekend was elk stew and room temperature bulgur with way too many onions and no parsley.

"Don't you see, that the reason bulgur has parsley is to offset any bad breath from onions," I tell my father.

"And how do you define, 'bad breath?'" he asks me, smiling.

The brothers drove me on their snowmobile somewhere far away and ordered French fries and hot chocolate.

How did those two always seem to know what I wanted?

I never saw that boat again but I did ride regularly on their snowmobiles.

Anyway, I saw them drink. Lots of times. I saw them drink ginger ales and cocoa. Probably now they are just deranged. Probably now they do drugs. Some sort of wild, ultra-hydrating drugs that make drinking liquids impossible. Probably now they are in some perpetual drug-induced, overly hydrated state. Maybe they are passed out for that reason right now which is why they are not up, watching me.

SATURDAY

Frank and Joe come up this morning, early, to avoid Friday night traffic. We hear their car in the drive. They bring rolls and buns from a bakery they pass on their way. The kids are still sleeping. Sue makes coffee and I start putting the breads on a platter, but suddenly I feel very tired. Sue looks at me and says that I have a rash on my neck and that I need to lie down. Joe follows upstairs, covers me with the quilt, whispers he is happy to be here, says he and Frankie are off to wire the property, and plants a warm kiss on my forehead. I fall asleep, thinking of how I should have mentioned Chris and Dave, and wonder if Joe and Frank will come across something this afternoon, the tent or the brothers, or whoever those two men really are.

Later I walk downstairs and am surprised to find out it is already late afternoon. The kids are at Marie's. Frank and Joe are back from wiring the property and are out back, chopping wood. Sue, at the sink, asks me if I feel ok.

I ask if our husbands are finished wiring.

She says yes and, again, asks if I feel better and if I want some coffee.

I nod yes to both.

We hear a knock at the front door. We walk together and open it. There are two men standing outside of it. The brothers, looking fit and well groomed.

"Hi," they say at the same time.

Sue puts her hand on her hip (she has sizeable hips but a tiny waist) and says, "Well, hello."

"Hi," they repeat.

I stand silent, unable to utter a single word. Sue's shirt is tied up at the waist and unbuttoned low. You can see the top part of her bra, a lacey, forest green.

"We wanted to come and say hello."

"Have a seat outside and I'll get our boys. Boys," Sue shouts out of the window above the sink, "we've got company."

Sue has had two children and has a fantastic stomach. She knows it. It is not the overly developed, muscular, kind, but soft, creamy and unwrinkled. I can't believe she chooses this time to show it off.

No one pays any attention to me. I stand in one place, not moving, not talking, and holding onto the front door. What do Chris and Dave want, coming here? It used to be they just wanted me. I went into their world, they did not come into mine. They had no interest in my family except for listening to the things I said about them. I am losing them. This makes me feel gray and toxic, like my car's gas tank; oily, like my car's engine, and my head throbs.

Chris and Dave turn away from the front door, walk to the outdoor table, and sit down, legs spread wide, on our wooden lawn chairs. Sue and I stand at the door, looking at them. Frank and Joe are still in the back. We hear them chopping wood.

"Boys," Sue says loudly, hand again on her hip, which she juts out, "We need y'all here, now."

"Where do you think you are, some cowboy movie?" I want to ask, but don't. She is really irritating me. Bouncing around in front of these brothers.

We hear the chopping stop.

Chris takes a small urn out of his pocket and sets it on the table separating him from Dave.

"What is that?" I ask, pointing to the small brass urn.

"Our Uncle" answers Dave. "He used to talk to us but he started lying and lost that power."

Frank and Joe, sweaty, walk around the cabin to greet the brothers.

Sue motions for me to come to the kitchen. I lean heavily against a counter.

I want to be with the boys but I do not want them here. I want to be alone with them away from here. Separate.

We cannot hear Joe and Frank and Chris and Dave out front. Our kitchen sink window overlooks the woodpile. We see an axe buried in a stump and several different-sized piles of neatly chopped wood: large logs, logs split in half, and smaller slices for kindling. We have a cupboard with family crystal and china. Once a year we empty it, rinse each glass, cup, bowl, plate, and clean the entire cupboard. Right now we are washing the wine glasses. "I sure like those two," Sue whispers, dunking the glasses in sudsy water. Her face is flushed.

At this point it is important for me to behave as if I do not like, or at least have no interest, in the brothers. So I do not say what I am thinking which is this, "Me too. I like them too. I like them a lot. And they used to like me. We have a history." Instead I ask, "Why?"

"I don't know," she smiles. "They are, different."

"They say they are actors," I whisper.

"How do you know?"

"They told me."

"You mean you have spoken to them?" she asks.

"Uhm, well yes, with Don, yesterday, in the woods."

"You DID? Why didn't you say?"

Joe, Frankie, and our visitors sit on the table outside of our porch, not talking. Chris pulls out a deck of cards and asks if anyone wants to play hearts.

Frankie and Joe say, "Sure."

We had planned to drive to a farm and get meat to store in our freezer. We agree to do that another time. It does not seem like a good idea to leave right now. There is a lot to do. We stand in the kitchen, listening to the men play cards. The windows are open and we don't hear a lot of conversation, just the slap of cards. It is not like Joe and Frankie to do something they do not want to do.

"We should bring them something," says Sue.

She fills a pitcher with water. She hands me four glasses, carries out the pitcher.

"Finally a good view," Chris says.

Joe and Frankie look at each other.

I pour water into the glasses. Joe and Frankie drink. Dave dips his fingers in the glass and daubs the moisture onto his cheeks and neck. Chris pours a bit of water from the glass onto his palms and rubs his hands, wrists, forearms together.

"Why are you doing that?" Sue asks.

I want to tell her. But Dave quickly answers.

"We can't drink."

"We absorb," adds Chris.

Both put their fingers inside the water glasses and moisten parts of their wrists and elbows.

"How can we help you?" asks Frankie.

Chris nods his head and starts talking. He explains they sleep here, in a tent, a ways inside the woods. He explains they hope we don't have a problem with that. They used to come here when they were boys, with their uncle. They add that this land is so big and unused, they do not see how we could mind them using it. And what is our problem with hunting? Seems we are happy enough to eat the elk and deer our neighbors catch on other property. What is it about ours? And we are voracious in our mushroom consumption. Why the double standard? He bends over and picks up a stick next to his chair. He starts drawing small circles in the dirt. Sue stands next to him. His head is bent down above her feet. She wears sturdy sandals.

"You have a nice belly but egads, your feet."

"Those are some fucking ugly shoes," adds Dave.

Sue draws her eyebrows together, flushes, and goes inside. I follow her, slowly, passing Dave. "Hey, we saw your mom in Scotland," he whispers in a way that no one but me can hear.

When we go back inside Sue is shaking. "What the hell? That was fucked up," she says, taking off her sandals and throwing them against the wall. Sue rarely swears. I see sweat on her upper lip. Buttoning up her shirt, and untying it at the waist, letting the tails hang in wrinkles over her blue jeans. She picks up the phone, "Good. Dial tone. And good our kids are not here. I think we should drive into town, talk to the police, and ask if they know about these creeps."

"They aren't bad, they are just actors," I say.

"How do you know?" she says.

We look outside, four men sitting quietly in chairs.

Both Frankie and Joe stand up. Chris says he needs a nap. All of a sudden both men lean their heads back in their chairs, start snoring. Frankie and Joe come into the kitchen. Even from inside, the snoring of the brothers is very loud. Sue and I suggest driving home or at least into town to report them to the police, but Frankie says running away would do no good and Joe says we have nothing to accuse them of.

We decide to do what we had already planned to do: leave the kids at Marie's and go to dinner in town at The Deer Street Inn.

And as long as we are in town, we might ask at the liquor store and gas station about the brothers. Although these places close at 6:30 so we might not have time. Still, a trip into town might help us find some things out about these brothers, maybe — I am hoping — enough to be able to stop worrying. We leave them snoring on our wood furniture next to our outdoor picnic table. It is our best choice under the current circumstances. We do not lock the door, because if anyone wants to get inside our cabin they can whether we lock it or not, and a locked door might express fear or suspicion. Once in the car I remember that I forgot to bring the mushrooms. Ron, the bartender of The Deer Street Inn, is interested in wild mushrooms and I try to bring them to him when we eat there. On my way back into the cottage to get them I take a quick look at the sleeping men. Both wear expensive looking camping shorts with several zippered pockets and have very muscular legs. They wear Italian tennis shoes that look to be brand new or are at least very clean. They sleep in the same position: head back, mouth slightly open, showing even, white teeth. I pick up my basket of mushrooms from our kitchen counter.

The Deer Street Inn is a big place with three different areas: dining hall, poolroom, and bar. We sit at the bar. I give Ron his mushrooms. He smiles and says they better not be poison like last time. Joe stares at him and Ron tells him he is kidding. "That is my cousin, the poison master," Frankie says, slapping my shoulder.

Frankie asks Ron about Chris and Dave.

Ron has worked at Deer Street for ten years. His eyes are made small by the fat puffs around them. His wife was born and raised in this town. Chris and Dave do not sound familiar to him. He asks some of the wait-staff who say the same thing—Chris and Dave do not ring a bell. We take our drinks to a table, decompress. It is too late to go ask at the gas station or tackle shop. These businesses are now closed. We decide to enjoy being together, us four adults, without the children, without their interruptions we can talk. We eat from the bowl of peanuts on the table, and order burgers. Sue and I ask for coleslaw, our husbands ask for fries. Being away from the cabin gives us a reality check: yes, the presence of the brothers is weird. But they did not do anything. And we are not sure the police here like us. This could be a setup. They, and certain others, might even get some satisfaction if we seemed to be scared for no reason, or if some sort of damage was done to our property or us.

Frankie orders a round of shots.

I touch my tongue in my drink, and hand it to Joe. I've

already had a few beers and don't feel like getting unsteady.

"OK," Frankie yells, "HOME."

I wonder about the hotels in town. I wonder if we are unsafe at our cabin and should consider staying in one. I make a suggestion but Frankie keeps looking straight ahead, saying, "HOME."

"I'll drive," I say.

"No fucking way," says Frankie.

For a while we are all quiet.

"Maybe those two men are bats," I say. Everyone ignores me.

I repeat, "Maybe those two are bats."

Still, silence.

"How many beers did you have?" asks Joe.

"Don't you notice we hardly have any mosquitoes this year? Bats eat mosquitoes. Don told me today. And that he put up bat houses. Those two are not real people, maybe they are bats."

"Not actors?" asks Sue.

"Who or whatever they are they want to fuck with us. What they are relying on," says Frankie, "is our politeness and our fear. Well we are not as fucking polite as they fucking think and we are not scared of them and their bullshit."

When we drive up to the cabin the chairs are empty, the urn is gone.

We do not go upstairs but sit in the living room. I am on the couch, next to Joe. I cannot sleep. Sue sits in the armchair across from me, lightly snoring. I don't see Frankie. After awhile I walk out on the porch. The sky is filled with stars. The night is clear. The moon is full. Frankie walks toward the cabin.

He motions for me to walk down the steps to him. He grips my arm, between the shoulder and elbow, at the bicep. He grips it hard. He has a gun in one hand.

"We are not scared of them and we are stronger," he says.

"Frankie, what..."

"I didn't do any fucking thing. I just showed those bastards we have this gun and I know how to use it. They won't be back."

"You have a hot head."

"And you space out, never see anything you don't want to."

I think, but don't tell him, he is right. I go back into the cabin, shake Joe gently.

"Joe, come on. We are going upstairs to sleep."

"Ok" he says, and falls flat on the couch. Sue does not wake up. Frankie stands on the porch, arms by his side, still holding the gun.

I walk upstairs, alone, wish I could just fly away somewhere with the brothers, collapse on our bed.

When it comes to Frankie, Joe completely loses his personality. Frankie is very strong, even overpowering and Joe is taken in. Frankie never knows when he should stop, and Joe never stops unless Frankie tells him to. Frankie always pushes things too far and everyone including me lets him. He is never ashamed, never embarrassed. He has a right to everything.

The brothers always know when to stop, even if it is just at the edge of severe trouble.

Suddenly I see them sitting across from my bed, in chairs made by my grandfather. The urn is on the floor.

"Your cousin is a real prince," says Dave.

"He was always like that, even when he was little," says Chris.

"Did you really see our moms in Scotland?" I ask.

"Yes. Boy can your mom swing a golf club."

There is a pause.

"We are really sorry," says Dave.

"Did you come here and find out you like Sue better than me?"

"Sue is not you. Only you are you. Nice husband," says Chris.

I start to cry.

He continues, "Before you the only girls who ever liked us were dirty."

I cannot stop crying.

"You would have really liked our uncle," says Dave.

"Why couldn't I ever meet him?"

"He didn't want to meet you, he just liked looking at you. And he said that a long time ago, before he became a liar, that we could never take you with us, even if you wanted to come. He seemed to think you would want to."

"I do. I do want to. I want to come with you." I am still crying and I also feel sick and overheated.

"You can't."

"Ok," I tell them. "Ok. But promise me that you will never, ever, really leave."

"We are not good for you. Look at all you have."

"I don't have anything."

"But you do, you have everything."

"Look, you take it, you take all I have. I don't care."

"We want you and what you have, but we can never take it."

"You are all I have. You two. Without you I have nothing. I have nothing to ever think about.

"Look," I point to the jewel—green with splotches of red—that hangs from my neck. The brothers gave it to me years ago. The presence of the jewel is strange in these woods, with all of the dirt, rivers and trees; with people in flannel and thick coats and worn boots.

"We never gave you that," they say simultaneously.

"Yes you did," I tell them.

"No we did not," they both answer.

They approach the bed.

"Lie down," says Dave.

Lying down, I cannot remember ever touching either of them. Not Chris, not Dave. They stand on either side of the bed. I am in between them. Each leans down and places a mouth, just for an instant, on my upper inner leg. Chris on the right, Dave on the left. I feel a huge pressure, as if something is pushing down on me, then a light sting, not unpleasant.

"Permanent inoculation," both say.

"Our uncle told us to tell you not to worry about this weird-seeming situation. A more sensible outcome would have screwed everything totally up. Now stand up, we are taking a trip," says Dave.

They hold my hands. I am still crying. Each of them hands me a handkerchief. Both are plaid. "We got these for you in Scotland," says Chris. I wipe my eyes and nose, put the handkerchiefs in my breast pocket, stand up between them, balanced on the balls of my feet, fill my lungs, and we take off, through the wide open window.

The three of us fly upward, into a dark, star-studded sky. I point my toes until my ankles crack. The air is cool and moist and I fly in between them, looking down at the lake, our beach, our large cabin.

We do a synchronized flip.

A few stars appear in the sky. Then, among the stars appears something that looks like a massive, winged animal. At first I think it is going to approach us but it stays still. We are moving toward it. We do another flip and fly together gathering speed. I grip their hands tightly. We spin toward the ship, face it, suddenly stop.

I look at Chris, then Dave. Their eyes, with no particular expression, are not on me, but the large vessel resembling a bird.

"There is our ship," says Dave.

"We will never leave you," says Chris.

I want to talk but cannot. Something feels caught in my throat. The brothers let go of my hands, fly through what look like the eyes of the bird, leaving me alone, dangling above the lake, above our cabin to watch their ship turn its nose up and climb into the sky. I take the handkerchiefs out of my breast pocket and sob into them uncontrollably.

Someone shakes my arm. It is Joe. I am sweating. Both hand-kerchiefs are wadded in my left hand. Joe is dirty. He tells me I have slept the entire day, asks if I feel better. He tells me that he and Frankie just finished wiring the property. He is going to take a shower. Everyone was concerned because I slept a long time and the rash got worse but now it looks to be gone. He hands me a glass of water, says if I feel better, we will take Marie and the kids into town for dinner. He looks me square in the eye for a while without speaking. Then he talks in a low voice. "About your cousin, Frankie. I like him ok. But you know you made clear from the beginning that anyone who married you had to be friends, close friends, with Frankie. It is not always easy for me to be with him, you know. I am not so sure of things the way he is. That is why I love you. I can rely on you." He puts his hand on my cheek, rubs the jewel hanging from my neck between his thumb and forefinger. He continues to talk. He says that he really loves me and that each year he is with me he loves me more, and that he hopes he can grow and become better. I find this stream of language unbearable. "Joe," I say, kissing his chin and then lips, "Stop expecting so much of yourself; you talk like a man in a dream."

"I am," he answers. "I am a man in a dream. It is the best and the longest damn dream any man ever got to have."

3
BRY

*those words conveyed an extraordinary
joy, as if it were settled*
VIRGINIA WOOLF

I chicken out; start off trying to duplicate a sense of horror in James' ghost story, perhaps the eeriest, greatest, ghost story of all time, and totally change course. After all of that talk about creepy, my story is hardly frightening.

My first version is horrific, but writing it makes me feel so bad and gives me so many sleepless nights I change it. In that version, there is a forbidden romance between the cousins, unconsummated. Chris and Dave are truly menacing. Frankie, convinced he is protecting his family, shoots and kills the brothers with the family shotgun. He tells the narrator what he has done. She wants to believe him but is nagged by doubts: did he act in good faith or as the hothead she knew he could sometimes be? For a while the murder remains their secret. But then someone finds the bodies and a police investigation begins. She faces a painful decision: lie to the police (in which case she will torture herself forever) or tell the truth, risking a long trial and jail time for her beloved cousin (in which case she will also torture herself forever).

Something in me cannot go through with it; it might be a better story, even closer to James' vision, but it feels wrong for me to write and think about it that way. So I delete that version and rearrange everything into what precedes these pages, *Turn of the North* — a story that hints at things eerie but truly avoids any real negotiation with evil.

To me, *Turn of the North* is a love story.

The project gives me some new people to think about and to love. Frankie is very tall, dark and handsome. Joe is also handsome but fair-skinned and with a shorter, sturdier build. I really love Sue and could, honestly, use her in my life right now. But it is the brothers, Chris and Dave — muscular, bushy hair, piercing eyes — who really sink into me.

When it is finished I spend some time loving it, then understand I must move on. Otherwise I will just hold onto, and depend upon, it, leaving me in the same rut that got me started with triathlon training.

But how can I find another project? I decide to ask our older twins, the only people who know about *Harvest* and *Turn of the North*. I decide I will show them my notebooks with bad handwriting, crossed out passages, torn out pages. I am embarrassed by the contrast between my haphazard "system" and their carefully written notes on white index cards; their thin, sleek laptops, and scheduled productions. I call them while the younger twins are at school and Euge is at work, arrange for them to visit.

That early afternoon, they let themselves in, I hand them the notebooks, we hug. They apologetically rush off to a fundraising meeting, and promise to come by the next morning.

Right then I know I will never regret this decision. Already I sense a lightness of relief, as if just unloading some heavy luggage, carried alone for too long.

The next day I wake up early, take a swim by myself, in our rooftop pool, return home, shower, and stare out the window. It is a warm day in early fall. Euge and I walk the children to school, he continues on to work, I return home. The older twins have already let themselves in. When I walk through our door they stand up, give me a hug, hand me a bound document, explain they typed up and printed out *Harvest* and *Turn of the North* for them and for me.

"Mom, you are really, really good at this."
"No I am not."
"Yes you ARE."
"But I didn't do anything."
"Yes you did."
"I just interact with Ernest and with Henry, or with who I imagine those two to be."
"But you do it in a way that is really, well, you."

Euge and I have raised these young adults to be very kind to people they like.

"Dad would love these; why keep them secret?"

A few moments go by.

"What would happen if you write something without a great dead author?"

"But what for?"

"Because you can."

"But Ernest and Henry are not dead, they will never die. That is the thing about books."

"*Harvest* and *Turn of the North* would be amazing films."

I feel a lump in my chest, whisper, "Thank you."

"Promise us you will keep working."

"Sure."

They give me another hug, and say they have to set up for afternoon rehearsal, and leave.

I sit and stare out our window, wonder how hard it would be to make something up without Ernest or Henry.

I picture Bitty and try to imagine what she would say. She would say I allow my mind to wander, that I dip into self-pity. I hear her voice, picture her outfit: white pants, red v-neck sweater, metallic, peep-toe heels. I think: what if I try to write as Bitty, or as I imagine she might write? Agitated, excited, I pull out an unused spiral-bound notebook from the chest of drawers in our dining room, stare at its unmarked pages. I replay Bitty, her voice, imagine what she sees, hears, am nearly overcome with a deep sense of foreboding: this will not work, it will not be good, it will wind up at the bottom of a chest of drawers or in an attic or incinerator. But I remind myself this project is not about distinction, it is about expression; it is an airing out. I pick up my pen and, with clear purpose, set to work on something that, I believe, contains my vision, and Bitty's.

I start with a title, Bitty's birth name: Gertrude Janine.

SOURCES

BOOKS
Ernest Hemingway *The Sun Also Rises*
Henry James *Turn of the Screw*
Virginia Woolf *To the Lighthouse*

SONGS
Michael Franti and Spearhead "People in the Middle"
Ben Harper "Diamonds on the Inside"

Special Thanks to "The Thing About Hope Is…"
Pearson Custom Publishing, 2003,
Boston, Massachusetts, David McGrath editor,
where portions of "Harvest" appeared
(titled "Dayball") and markzine,
where Gertrude first appeared.

Lynn Crawford, a fiction writer and art critic, lives outside of Detroit with her family. Her previous books include: *Solow, Blow, Simply Separate People* and *Fortification Resort*. She is a 2010 Kresge Literary Arts Fellow and a founding board member of Museum of Contemporary Art Detroit.

The press and author would like to thank
University Cultural Center Association
in Detroit, Michigan for their
generous support of
this publication.

Simply Separate People, Two is printed in an edition of 750 copies. The text is set in Perpetua type. Futura appears on the title page and cover. Thomson-Shore of Dexter, Michigan printed and bound the books.

FIRST EDITION